UNFAIR WINDS

CAMILLE DUPLESSIS

OLIVERHEBERBOOKS

Published by Oliver-Heber Books

0 9 8 7 6 5 4 3 2 1

 Created with Vellum

AUTHOR'S NOTE

The story in these three books was meant to start as more of a chamber piece, then focus on the ensemble of characters as everybody eases into loving and being loved. This third installment is an ending of sorts... at least to the initial arc of this trilogy and *The Kraken and The Canary*. It opens a month after *The Only Story* finishes. Before you dive in, I'll gently point out a few content-related things, as I did in the first book: addiction is still a theme, as is bereavement. There are allusions to emotional abuse and potential violence, as well. None are graphic or dominate the page.

Strong loves end in grief, as far wiser people than me have said in more lyrical ways. I've experienced said grief as a proportionate, loud echo, so the thought had more of an impact as I ideated and wrote. "Happily ever after" can be found in choices and moments, which is a strong idea woven into *Unfair Winds*. I did want people to be happy, but this is also everyone at certain points in time.

And if it wasn't obvious, I'm annoyingly attached to places I've evoked. They're mostly actual sites. However, my eye is more on feelings than historical immersion. If I've roused your interest in facts, there are *many* brilliant things to consult. Primary sources have been digitized by the Norfolk Records Office, and oodles of books are available through shops like The Book Hive and Inanna's Festival. Both are staffed by lovely people (special mention to Gaz!) who are a wealth of information themselves.

I hope N never gets sick of these dedications. Here's another one with all the love in my dark little heart.

1

JUNE, 1901

Cromer

"I don't *know* what will happen after I see the grave. I've already told you." Paul slathered his toast with marmalade and took a large bite.

If he had been a hopeful man, he would swear he caught Alastair's amused chuckle. Benson tutted when marmalade dribbled to the table.

But Paul heard nothing from beyond the grave, which made him the minority party in his own establishment. That was just the trouble: Benson's pet topic of late *was* Alastair. Whether Paul could sense him, or had seen something about visiting his resting place.

The resounding *no* to both lines of inquiry had been the same for a good thirty days, the amount of time which had passed since Lennie's misguided stepbrother had held Paul at knifepoint. Things had been brought into sharp relief, and he'd finally decided to visit his beloved's grave. He knew its location now, thanks to the help of a nosy selkie. Theo hadn't been asked to help; he'd simply disappeared for a bit and returned bearing the information.

Paul forced himself to chew and swallow. He half-prayed he'd just choke and answer Benson's queries eloquently by dying. It might be his luck that wherever he ended up himself, it wouldn't be with Alastair. He met Benson's stare as though challenging him to mention the marmalade dribble.

Benson wouldn't. He was an incarnate mass of soiled rags. Anyway, Paul would clean all the tables later this morning. He'd never missed a day doing it, not when it was his task to complete rather than Tom's or a maid's. The Shuck might not be the most opulent of places. He felt it becoming more of a relic as the world so rapidly progressed. But it was among the cleanest.

"Liar."

He shrugged. He couldn't lie about what he couldn't see.

A seer who saw nothing was as knowledgeable as somebody who'd never had the sight at all.

Although Benson called him a witch of sorts, they both supposed he was more accurately a seer. Either way, Paul couldn't say if he preferred this blunted state or his previous one. It did feel like he possessed a phantom limb, regardless. He also knew he hadn't seen the point in nursing a talent that had failed him.

So, he let it wither. Shortly after Alastair's son arrived to ultimately take him away, Paul decided to ignore the things he'd usually allow himself to see. Much as training himself to see them, pretending they didn't exist took practice.

He hadn't made his choice obvious, not to anybody. He preferred instead to allow everyone to assume he still had premonitions and could access the strange ether that had once kept each of his feet in separate realities. He'd chosen to be a landlord, not a seer, and the latter identity had languished until Tom returned to work with him.

After clearing his throat, Benson gave Paul another look that was presumably meant to goad him into speaking more. They presently sat at a table in the quiet taproom. It was a matter of routine, not genuine good humor. Benson often took breakfast with Paul, and he should have known better than to goad him, for it rarely worked.

"You *really* don't have a sense of what's coming next?" Benson sipped tea with no milk, *with* brandy in one of his own chipped, dirty cups. The tea induced winces; the cups begged questions about their own structural integrity and hygiene.

Regardless of the brew's potency, Benson's bister eyes were weary, belying late nights with Mr. Mills studying who knew precisely what. David still mostly resided in Norwich, but he'd been here many times in the last month. Secreted away in Benson's stale room learning the intricacies of witchery and, Paul suspected, a type of benign necromancy nobody wanted to bring up near him. The person whom he'd loved most was dead, currently a wraith trapped in The Shuck, and the reason for such explorations.

Tom wouldn't talk about what sort of tutelage David received: he felt sorry for his uncle. Theo wouldn't address it because the selkie was too genteel to cause undue distress. Lennie wouldn't, because they followed David's lead on the matter, and David seemed too harried and busy to explain anything at all. Of everyone involved, David would be the best person to confront apart from Benson, who was proud and peevish as a tomcat venturing outdoors.

In Benson's case, neither decency nor manners motivated his silence. Rather, fear was the culprit. Paul saw it in his slightly furtive movements, in his uncharacteristic distrust of empty corners. Apparently, it mattered little if the ghost in question was an old friend. If anyone had an aversion to specters, it was Benson, which was unfortunate. He was the most knowledgeable about them.

Paul thought back to his childhood, almost all of it spent in this public house if he was not at school or wandering the shore or the promenade, and all the truths he'd kept obscured—he'd never seen ghosts to his knowledge. But he'd had so many visions of the future he'd needed to keep from his younger brother.

Edward had known almost everything about him except for that, and it was Mother and Father who encouraged Paul not to say anything. He understood why. But in retrospect, he did feel Edward would have been less bothered than they'd assumed. In time, *they* weren't even so bothered, for Paul had been able to avert a modest handful of small disasters involving things like theft and injury.

Sighing, he rubbed at the bridge of his nose. Now he just kept a different sort of secret. He felt it wearing thin. "Really. Truly. Nothing." Paul eyed the tabletop between them, then let his gaze drift to Benson's filthy waistcoat. Early morning, June light underscored stains on the fabric, which had once been bottle green.

He wouldn't elaborate upon how he'd left his foresight alongside his dead husband, and he still referenced his ability in the present tense. It made things easier because he did not have to untangle his grief for others to digest. Or receive their sympathy.

Sympathy, he suspected, would paralyze him. This little family that'd somehow coalesced in his pub did require he remain reasonably functional. He was equally determined not to succumb to his usual bout of yearly melancholy, though had yet to cross that bridge. Worst of everything because it merely fed Paul's guilt, Lennie seemed greatly encouraged to find a fellow seer in Paul.

After making their acquaintance, Paul was even more reluctant to admit the reality that for years, he'd been almost as numb to future outcomes as any person who'd never had the sight. But things still badgered for his attention. He felt he would never shed the nagging, though he'd done a thorough job ignoring the rest. But when things nagged, they were hazy sights in an ancient looking glass and no longer the immersions he'd once experienced as a boy and younger man.

"Nothing at all?"

"Nothing."

After a moment of pause and bestowing him with one weighty sigh, Benson said, "If you're that oblivious, it's little wonder you can't sense Alastair now."

Paul knew he was being needled. "I've *never* been sensitive to ghosts. Just the future. Which, if you're talking to him, he'll be able to tell you."

"There's still something you're not saying," Benson pressed. "David's abilities have improved. *And* The Shuck isn't bewitched now."

It wasn't, Paul knew. He felt far less like he was walking through invisible, delicate silk scarves dangling from the ceilings and crossbeams. He had grown so used to brushing them aside that the sensation of doing so long stopped bothering him. But once it was gone, he noticed its absence.

Benson continued, "What's causing the interference now?"

Paul glanced at the empty air to Benson's left,

above his head, where Alastair's eyes could be met if he stood by Benson's chair. "You should tell Benson to shove off, love. I've no interest in this." But he did. He had an interest, and envy, because his interest could not transmute into an ability. The days since Robbie's desperate break-in had eased the furious red chafing on his throat. But time had not mellowed his yearning, just like it hadn't lessened the utter need that was unearthed when he considered his beloved might be within the same room. Veiled from his perception by some act of God or the cosmos.

"That's where he's standing!" said Benson. "*Something* in your bloody stubborn hindbrain must be connected to him."

"All the same, I don't care what's causing anything. Business is better. Isn't that all I needed out of David, or anyone?"

Once he realized his love was for men, he had no interest in worshipping a God whose loudest followers often claimed he was bound for hell. Whatever kept him and Alastair apart, and he wanted to believe it was less religious than preternatural, he hated and didn't understand it.

"He says you're lying about not caring."

"Oh, he says, does he?"

Benson did not confront that directly, just as he chose not to engage with so many things. "And he says you've a flat full of letters to him."

With a disgruntled huff, Paul asked, "So what if I do?" He'd never mentioned it, yet couldn't be shocked that Benson possessed the knowledge.

"If you leave them out for him to read, he will. But you cover 'em up and hide 'em away."

Paul felt if anyone else read them, it would be like running around naked. Too vulnerable, too cold.

Though Theo had been in the flat numerous times to balance the books and tend to the various accounts kept in Paul's minuscule office, Paul had taken cautions to keep his private endeavors from eyes other than his own.

Regardless, the letters weren't anything. Not a novel, not a book. Just words upon words written as though Paul were a boy keeping a journal or commonplace book.

He had friends; Alastair hadn't been his only one. But Alastair always heard everything, minutiae and any matters of import. Nearly every day since the third week after they'd taken Alastair's coffin, he'd written something. It was often very simple—the weather, a comical thing some drunk had uttered, an old client of Mrs. Lloyd's asking if she'd consider taking him back, finding a new way of brewing.

"Can't he just take them out for himself, if he's here?"

"No," said Benson. That was intriguing. "David's bewitchment held him back for years. He's still learning how to do more than lurk. Making progress, though."

"He can do more than lurk?" Paul abhorred the hope in his voice.

"Some of them can." The sentence held promise.

Paul didn't ask for deeper specificity. "Fine, I shall leave some of the papers uncovered."

"You might be surprised if you do. He wants to communicate with you," said Benson. An earnestness that had laced through his words for the last few weeks rested in his speech. "Maybe there's a detail that'll help him." Sitting back, Benson squinted at him. "Do you still dream? You told me it was how you got many of your premonitions."

"Don't sleep well enough to dream, now." Before Alastair, and while they were together, premonitions had often come to him as he slept.

He hadn't slept properly for quite some time, although he used to sleep well and with gusto. A bit of his insomnia was, he suspected, age and all the differences it brought to the mind and body.

Some of it, however, must have resulted from his attempts to truncate his abilities. His sleep *had* certainly worsened when he decided to be just a landlord who'd never peered beyond the veil with powers of precognition. He could still sense preternatural beings: he'd known at the start of their acquaintance that Theo was not what he seemed. Benson and David felt alike. Tom felt like him, a little. Lennie more so.

But whatever link he'd had to precognition was broken. Perhaps that had more consequences than he'd anticipated.

"Try to sleep better. Ghosts love to invade dreams." Benson sipped. "The bastards. They love it almost as much as jumping into your body and controlling it like a puppet."

For a moment, the idea of receiving something from Alastair through a dream was seductive. "I can try... doesn't mean it'll happen." If he didn't open himself back up, he doubted it would be possible, and if he couldn't see Alastair in dreams, he doubted he could be controlled like a puppet. If he couldn't accomplish the more passive thing—sleeping to dream —he couldn't imagine the more intense one.

Or are they both passive if the ghost is taking charge? For a second, Paul found the notion of possession tantalizing. It might feel similar to being sexually dominated, and even beyond that, if Alastair could be so close to him after years of separation... he sighed.

After a pause and a deeper sip, Benson said, "David is here again, tonight. He's said he wants to move back, only there's the business to think of and..." he waved a grizzled hand, his silver rings catching the sun as he did, and Paul had to smile. Only a man who had never had such responsibilities or wealth could be so dismissive. "I told him some things are more important."

"I think he should come back. But you can't dissuade him from his work, you know. We've all got our roles, haven't we?"

"What's yours, then?"

As the smile faded from Paul's face, he answered first with another exceedingly sloppy bite of toast. Then he said thickly, "Widowed father figure."

"Christ, that's grim."

Paul didn't think so, but it was lonely. He endeavored to do something about that loneliness besides read, or go for aimless walks, or try to solve others' problems, for the first time in years. Tonight—this afternoon, really, when Tom arrived—Paul was going to get very pissed.

Everyone else had sought such solace and it was high time he took his turn. This was all too much, and he did not know what to do about any of it.

~

"Stubborn boy," Alastair said. "Stubborn, beautiful, ridiculous boy."

David watched as Alastair tried to pace the secondhand rug on Benson's floor. But because he was the ghost of a formerly muscular man and the room was somewhat narrow, it could only be called pacing in a generous sense. In point of fact, it was scuffling.

Additionally, David felt it might be hyperbolic to call Paul a boy. Then, Alastair had been older than him by a decade or so. Habits were hard to break.

David shifted a little from his perch on Benson's narrow bed. Despite a month's worth of meetings in his small room, he still couldn't get used to the state of the place. He tried to be polite and hadn't seen any bedbugs, so it wasn't inordinately difficult to keep his peace. There was just nowhere to sit except for the permanently disheveled bed, a rattan chair that looked like it might buckle, or a squat, splintered table strewn with dirty dishes and a broken astrolabe.

"He's keeping something from us," said Alastair.

Intrigued, David eyed the toe of Alastair's boot when it appeared to catch the rug's edge. "Did you feel that?" It was new. He did not wish to interrupt the flow of Alastair's musing, but wanted to gauge how physical things felt to him.

During one of the most grueling months of his life, David had managed through Benson's eccentric and helpful schooling to endow a ghost with more life. Benson said he was a conduit, channeling essence and ability to Alastair. All David felt was exhaustion and elation.

First, he'd felt like he was talking to either empty space or a slightly responsive shadow. Then, gradually, yet more quickly than he'd have imagined, the shadow became more human and realistic.

Now, he saw a lovely man who would have terrified him a year or two ago. Dressed in black. On the taller side, and built like he'd scrapped his way through life. Heavily tattooed on visible spans of skin. Masses of dark hair strewn with gray. There was something poetic in his demeanor, overall.

Upon hearing David's description, Benson said

this was Alastair shortly before his death. So David took him at his word, although there was no known way to prove they each saw the same person.

"What?"

When Alastair's worn boot caught the rug again and he impatiently freed it like anybody would, David said, knowing he could feel it due to how he reacted, "That."

"Oh, the rug? Could kill someone, you know, a poorly placed rug. Years ago, now, this odious bastard called Sykes wanted to knife me. But he fell *arse over tit* because he was pissed and a rug was..." Alastair swallowed, halting himself, and met David's eyes.

David smirked.

Alastair grinned. "Shit, how long have I been doing that?"

"Only just now, that I've seen. I wonder if, because we take so much for granted about living while being alive, our brains..." David frowned. Alastair's had long rotted away. "Your brain is used to when you were alive, so maybe you just didn't notice when you started doing it again. It's like... when someone has a leg amputated, oftentimes they still feel the leg, don't they?"

Maybe it wasn't like that at all.

"Never mind," said Alastair, and he came to sit on the bed next to David. For the first time, David felt his weight when he settled.

"What do you think Paul is keeping from us? If there's no more bewitchment, then what's the trouble? I mean to say, I'm sure he holds back a lot, but do you have any idea?"

"Well..."

He studied Alastair's profile, pensive and soft in the gaslight. Paul wasn't interested in electricity, or so he said. Luckily, gas suited The Shuck. Even David, who was more used to venues with electric light, generally disliked the stark illumination it provided. "Would it help you if we helped him?

It seemed true that ghosts often lingered because they had left behind an unsolved problem, and evidently they could become more tenacious about it over time. Even Lennie had started to see Alastair here and there, as had a scattered few customers. Meanwhile, the person Alastair wanted most in the world seemingly had no awareness of his presence.

David waited for Alastair to speak, having learned he disliked being prodded or interrupted too many times. Benson didn't care about Alastair's conversational preferences, but he was often somewhat drunk when they interacted anyway.

Glancing at the door, David wondered when he'd be back. He'd said something about an errand, but David wasn't fooled: though David took to channeling like a duck in water, Benson himself noticeably shied away from the practice. Little errands kept cropping up for Benson, of late.

"Don't know. He said he couldn't see anything in the future, this morning. When Benson was pressing him." Alastair had taken to following Benson whenever he went to talk to Paul, and David couldn't blame him.

"Is that odd, though?" David hadn't had many discussions about foresight, but he did know premonitions weren't always biddable. And even if someone had a knack for them, it took practice and dedication to follow them, understand what they meant, and sift through them when asked a question. "Maybe he just can't. Aren't there fallow periods, sometimes?"

He did not know what a seer would rather a period

without any premonitions be called. Seers weren't exactly farmers.

"For him? Not that I knew of."

"So... he never mentioned them just... abating. Then, I don't know. Coming back again."

"Never," said Alastair, chewing just a little at his lower lip in thought. He brightened momentarily. "Fuck, I can feel my *teeth* again." David chuckled, and Alastair's expression straightened as he appeared to think. "They just happened. He was very good at functioning *when* they happened, but I know he dreamt them often. He used to talk in his sleep when he did." Alastair smiled, almost to himself; David found it endearing.

"Then it *would* be strange for him to say he's seen nothing." It was more of a statement than a question. "Well, what about age? Perhaps he's just aging, as we all have to."

As soon as he said it, he realized that couldn't be it, either. David hadn't read quite as much about seers as he had ghosts, but everything he'd perused claimed seers' abilities might intensify over time.

Reason dictated, if reason could be applied to the preternatural, that Paul would be having *more* visions in his middle age.

It seemed Alastair had the same conclusion. "No, in all the stories I ever heard, anyone with the sight can become fucking insufferable. Some of them are like bloody Merlin, the older they get." He scrubbed at his face with both his hands. "He's so obstinate. He won't tell you. Even if he needs help or he's hurting, he won't say. He'll break first."

"Obstinate and private." David recalled that almost all he knew about Paul came from others until recently. He had felt so fortunate when Paul had told him how Alastair had come running into The Shuck, back then known as The Queen Anne, and asked for a hiding place. Tom hadn't known then and David didn't know if he knew now.

"Yes," mumbled Alastair, the sound slipping between his fingers. Then, he let his hands rest in his lap. "Fucking secretive, you mean." He drew a breath that served no purpose and released it.

An idea occurred to him that was almost sadder than any others he'd considered when it came to why Paul was so immune to Alastair's return. Despising the line of thought, David asked, "Do you know... so, if someone with the sight has to practice... or at least become accustomed to what they see..." he sighed. "Rather, I know that I managed to..."

"Just come out with what you're trying to ask." Overall, Alastair seemed remarkably patient, given his circumstances.

"Can they bury their abilities, too?" David had buried his own, after all. Until recently, he'd kept his own talents so segmented from his daily life that they hardly existed in practice. David's reasons were very likely different from Paul's, related to his own rigid upbringing rather than bereavement. But Paul might have done the same as David out of sorrow.

Minor aspects of magic had always leaked from him, even before the last six months or so when he had been thinking more about it. He understood that, now. It hadn't been until Theo told David of his identity that David began embracing his own witchery. Prior to then, he might see glimmering threads between people, and he sometimes sensed truths before being told about them. His repression was thorough, for until he gave up his denial, he rationalized these things into tricks of the light or a decent intuition.

Then even more witchcraft had come leaking out of him when he'd accidentally stunned Lennie's stepbrother with the briefest touch. It seemed repression could only do so much when he was pushed.

He watched as Alastair considered his question. Its answer was an eloquent and horrified, "Oh, fuck me."

Before David could reply, Benson threw open the door. He said, "Well, our Paul is off to Edinburgh in the morning. Can't stand the lot of us, I guess. And he's drunk, first time I've ever seen it."

He did break first, David thought, ruefully.

2

———

It wasn't the first time in recent memory that David had shown up on their doorstep long after the day's work had concluded. But this time, he had evidently consumed no spirits and his rationale seemed sound. His footsteps were even. Tom let the curtain fall back against the window after he had verified who knocked, then he wrenched open the door. With a sigh, he gestured for David to come inside.

"What is it, a fire at The Shuck? Doubt there's anything I can do about it from here. May as well let it burn."

His levity wasn't appreciated, if David's peeved expression was any indication. "Your uncle is running off to Scotland tomorrow morning. He slipped out this afternoon and purchased the tickets. While you were keeping the bar."

"He... pardon?"

Tom knew the journey was probably in the back of Paul's mind. It had been, probably, since Lennie's stepbrother cornered him in his flat. But because Paul embarked on most things with a deliberate pace, Tom hadn't thought about the possibility of an abrupt departure. He'd assumed all the circumstances and plans would be discussed so that everyone would have an equal idea of what might come next. The very last thing he would have foreseen was Paul dashing up to Edinburgh without warning.

He shut the door behind David and tried to look less startled.

When Theo joined them, Tom glanced at him, unbothered that he was barely half-dressed and clutched merely an old pair of trousers at his svelte waist. David had seen everything Theo had to offer, anyway, and more to the point, they'd all seen each other naked.

Tom asked Theo, "Did Paul say anything about it yesterday when you were upstairs with the books?" Their cottage was small enough, and Theo's hearing good enough, that Tom trusted Theo had overheard everything and needed no explanation. He had enough firsthand knowledge of selkies to understand their hearing was, in a word, excellent.

"No, nothing," said Theo. Then, he appeared to consider something. "But he does know where Alastair's grave is. He finally asked a few days ago and seemed quite relaxed about it. Well, relaxed for Paul. I thought little of the question; I was just happy he asked." It was in Portobello Cemetery, which was not one of the older places of burial in the area, but a rather modern one.

Trying to make sense of the sudden choice, Tom redirected his attention to David. "Did anything happen to prompt him to do it? To decide now?" He put on the shirt he'd left draped over one of the chairs by the fireplace, thankful he hadn't yet shed his trousers. "*Right* now."

"I can't say. I only just found out and thought you needed to know. Who else would run the pub but you? He's dead set on going; I cornered him on my way out. Thankfully, he's a happy drunk."

Tom scoffed and met David's gaze. He would likely have died for those eyes once, but was pleased he had grown up. He assessed the haphazard state of David's trilby and his unbuttoned coat, deciding there indeed must be something underfoot.

"There's more, Tom."

Wary, Tom said, "What else can there be?"

"He's not just pissed, if you want my measure. I don't think we can stop him from leaving, and perhaps we shouldn't. But I don't know if he should be trusted to go on his own, if you catch my meaning."

The implications seemed clear. Tom didn't doubt a man who was intoxicated could make deadly decisions. *I did.*

Self-harm wasn't in Paul's nature, unless one counted deep seclusion and silence as harmful. But the last few weeks had been unprecedented for all of them. There was no telling precisely how he felt now; Paul kept his emotional states ambiguous to outsiders under the most normal of conditions.

Of anyone in his family, blood or found, Tom was the resident drunk who drowned in his emotions. Rather, he had been. He was proud of a string of months free of constant, daily inebriation. Having given absolute sobriety a go and discovering he needed to wean himself even more slowly than he'd first believed, he was still happy to have avoided using drink as religiously as he once had.

While Paul had never been a teetotaler, neither was he prone to drinking to excess. As Tom sifted through the dismay all this brought, for Paul hadn't ever imbibed so much even in the depths of his grief,

Theo placed a gentle palm on his arm. Soft warmth flowed through Tom's shirtsleeve, stilling his mind.

"We can go there directly," Theo said. "After I put on a shirt."

"All right," said Tom, kissing him on the cheek before he disappeared. He asked David, "Is Lennie here, too?"

"No, they're at home. Joining me on Saturday."

"Shame. They're Paul's favorite, you know."

At that, David beamed. "I know. It's quite something, is it not? I'm happy they both get on so well. But they're phenomenal at managing the—well, everything. Accounting, reconciling..." Tom found it impossible not to smile, too, as David visibly caught himself from going on. "Just been leaving them to business, these last few times I've met with Benson and Alastair."

At times, or truly, most of the time, Tom couldn't comprehend how his former lover was suited to rubbing shoulders with ghosts. But he still had to admit the shifts in David's demeanor were all for the better. Perhaps death really was the great equalizer, for in life, he couldn't picture a man like Alastair dealing with a man of David's type. Unless something unsavory was involved in the interaction.

One, a relatively genteel smuggler turned co-landlord, and the other, an educated lad with too many good manners and possibly too much money. New money, money from a business that spanned only three generations of family, but money all the same. Though, Tom admitted he should not make assumptions about Alastair being poor, as he supposed one could become quite comfortable though illicit means.

"How is that progressing?"

Tom had only seen Alastair twice in mirrors. Both

times he had dropped what he held, having been so startled. The first time it had been tea, which made a right mess despite the cup's survival, and the second time it had been a modest pile of books, which bruised his toes even through his boots.

"Sometimes I can't believe it myself. It's just like talking to you. I *have* always done it, though."

Tom nodded, recalling so-named imaginary friends that David referenced a few times. They had very likely been specters, especially if this present aptitude was anything to judge by. "You just squished it all down."

Like he'd done to everything soft, odd, or vulnerable in his life.

"Yes, well," said David, looking incredibly like the man Tom had known longer than the one David was now. Put out, vaguely displeased. Then it passed from his face. "I like him. He's bracing. And he's starting to be more corporeal. I don't know the correct word for it. He's feeling things, now."

Impressed, Tom asked, "How do *you* feel, though?" This was all beyond the realm of what he knew and could do, so he was curious if David was suffering fatigue or strange effects. To Tom, it seemed rather like Alastair was some manner of vampire, feeding off David's energy or health: not with any malicious purposes, but because Tom just assumed that was how a relationship between them had to work.

"Energized. Exhausted. I'm tired from all the back-and-forth between here and Norwich, and the later nights... and probably something mystical. But beyond that? It feels good."

It wasn't what Tom expected, but he was glad to hear it all the same. "Good. But you seem as surprised as me."

"The way Benson was talking of mediumship, I worried I'd be half-dead by now."

"He's always been frightened of ghosts. I expect it's made him talk more severely. I don't know if something happened to him to make him so nervous. But it's not an uncommon fear, is it?" If anything, the number of cautionary ghost stories had to be evidence of a fear held by many people. But they were quite matched by an ongoing zeal for spiritualism, so Tom couldn't say. Benson never called himself a spiritualist, or a medium, or anything of the kind.

Privately, Tom wondered if the categories were really so discrete from witch, witch-hunter, or seer.

"And just because Benson and I can do the same things, it doesn't mean we'll have the same strengths. Or experiences."

"When did you get so wise?"

"Oh," said David, and he actually winked. "Sometime when you weren't looking."

"Well, let us go rescue him," said Theo, reentering the room fully dressed, putting both Tom and David to shame despite the errand being both irregular and well past anyone's normal hours. Tom silently admired how the maroon of his greatcoat offset his brown eyes. Theo's only concession to all the irregularity was his lack of any kind of hat, and his dark hair glowed warm in the candlelight.

"All right," sighed Tom.

He hoped it would be the first and last time he ever came to Paul's rescue, but sensed it wouldn't be the last at all.

~

NOTHING FELT RIGHT.

Tom had never felt so askew in The Shuck despite initially wanting nothing to do with it and only returning at his mother's urging. It had always felt welcoming to him, even if he had not wished to be there at all. He didn't know if it felt so unsettled because of what he knew: Paul was drunk and rather manically packing for a sojourn north, and neither of these factors fit with Paul's established standing as a Miss Havisham-like figure—or if the building itself was nervous about its keeper's state.

Theo sometimes spoke of The Shuck as a person or an entity and never had that been so apparent to Tom as it was these days. *Or,* he thought, watching his uncle cast clothes into a carpetbag without a care for what exactly they were or how they were arranged, *is it Alastair who feels so...* he couldn't find a precise word.

The air rested on tenterhooks like a dark sky that threatened an immense downpour. He imagined a ghost could make a place feel so charged, and had it on two witch-hunters' authority that the resident ghost was displeased.

"Paul?" He'd said Paul's name twice already in the last forty seconds. He took a breath and steeled himself, noting that Paul's usual scent of birch tar, not at all of the physical world, was fainter than usual.

Do I fetch his physician? Tom didn't think it was a wise idea, though. Dr. Jones was kindly and knew Paul well enough. He just wasn't versed in what really ailed him.

This time, Paul did look up. Luckily, as David had said, he was indeed a cheerful if chaotic drunk. "Yes?"

"I'm going with you."

"Where?"

"To Scotland."

Tom had taken it upon himself to go up and speak

with his uncle. He had briefly relayed his tentative travel plans to both David and Theo before doing so. Since nobody felt Paul should go alone, Tom decided on the walk over that he would leave as well. Theo could remain at The Shuck to tend to the place, David and Lennie could keep to their usual schedules, and Benson, who was always underfoot anyway unless he paid a visit to his brother, would try to assuage Alastair.

Evidently, he was *very* unnerved by Paul's instability. Benson announced it almost immediately when Theo and Tom came in, but David's pained wince confirmed to Tom it was true.

"Alastair *is* definitely shouting," was all David had said. By the look on his face, the shouting was either livid or obscene. Both, perhaps.

"I'll be perfectly fine on my own."

"Will you?"

Paul smiled and rolled up a puce scarf before lowering it into the carpetbag. "Yes."

"Not to sound too dire, but, I've never seen you like this."

"Worried I will do myself a violence, are you?"

Peering at him, Tom couldn't help but wish to tell the truth. Paul wasn't his only family member left, especially if he counted Theo, David, and Lennie or even Benson and Mrs. Lloyd. But seeing as his stepfather could not tolerate his presence, he had been effectively alienated from his mother. She'd initially suggested he return to work here under the pretense of Paul needing the help, rather than at the pub that had once been his father's.

Yet she and Tom both knew it was predominately because her second husband disliked, and disapproved, of him.

Although he visited his grandmother's and his father's graves with nothing but love, he'd greatly prefer not to visit Paul's for a while yet, even if Apollyon men might have a predisposition for dying early. He often wondered if his own heart was bad, like Father's. Or even Alastair's, who was almost an honorary Apollyon. *If he and Paul could have actually been married, I wonder whose surname would have won.*

Tom blinked once, banishing the fanciful thought. "Yes. I *am* a bit worried."

The simple words seemed to reach Paul in a manner pontification could not. He stopped his disorderly packing and stepped over to Tom, who sat in a fawn button back chair angled toward the foot of the bed, and rested a hand on his shoulder.

"I wouldn't. I'm too frightened. I don't know what's coming next, you see?"

"You think you'll go to hell?"

The thought had never entered Tom's mind when he'd wanted to end himself. He'd thought blissfully of the cessation of endless sensations, of stopping the unrelenting thoughts following one after another like unruly and daunting motorcars. He had looked forward to peace. Fear had never been a consideration, although perhaps it should have been.

He searched his uncle's face. Paul's cheeks were slightly stubbled, his countenance so like Father's and Tom's own. Yet an untouchable quality always lingered within his expressions, as though some higher power had merely placed him upon earth to observe everyone else.

Tom couldn't decide if grief had caused the remoteness, or if it was something more innate. Loss had shaped Paul like water wore down stone. He knew little of his uncle before the process had commenced.

While Paul had spoke of fear, his eyes were still reasonably calm. "I don't believe in hell, first of all. Think I'm *in* hell, a lot of the time."

"Then what are you afraid of?"

"I suppose you'd understand better than most this sort of conversation."

Tom wasn't ashamed of his past choices. He shrugged. "Probably."

"You know, I am proud of you." Paul squeezed his shoulder gently.

"Proud?" It was the last thing he expected to hear.

"For being alive. It's dirty work, is living."

Letting pleasure at the recognition exist alongside his concern, he gently redirected the discussion. "What are you scared of?"

"That it won't be any different from now."

"That he won't be there even if you do die."

"Well, that, or... what if he is, and it still doesn't make any difference at all?" Paul shifted from where he stood and reached for a half-full, crystal glass of cognac sitting on a low table. He took a long drink, relieving the glass of a third of its contents. "He's here. But I go... wherever. We could be just... separated."

"I've seen him twice, and I'm closer to your sort of witch than David or Benson's kind. Don't give up," murmured Tom, finding no judgment at all for a man using whatever means possible to feel a bit less than what he felt.

The colors surrounding Paul appeared the same as ever, all the shadows of dark glens and trees. But he had such a strong sense of self that Tom couldn't quite use them as a reliable indicator of his private state in the manner he did with others. Paul did smell slightly more of sulfur, to Tom's nose. It could herald mental unrest as much as it could physical ailments.

Before Paul spoke again, he took another drink that left the glass two-thirds empty. "You're such a gentle soul. It's not him who poses the problem. He's trying. It's me. I'm not trying."

Puzzling over what he meant, Tom shook his head. "You're not the problem. He died, and you..." Tom didn't want to say it, but did. "Changed. There's no shame in that, none."

He supposed it would be less of an issue in his own future. Theo would outlive him. They both had others in their lives whom they loved, whom they understood and who understood them. Paul had friends, too, yet Tom didn't think he'd ever let anyone closer than Alastair. Tom still couldn't try to imagine his own life without Theo; it was too desolate of a picture. So he did understand Paul's desolation, at least.

Fondly, Paul said, "You're being kind. You could say I died when he died, or you could say I turned mean and cold and taciturn and odd. I wouldn't blame you at all." He fastened the carpetbag with steady fingers; Tom wondered if they shared a familial high tolerance for liquor. If he didn't know Paul was drunk, he'd just assume he was in a uniquely talkative, impulsive, and abstracted mood. "Changed is a lovely euphemism, however."

Sighing, knowing there'd be no reasoning with him, Tom rose and his eyes landed on a piece of slightly yellowed paper atop a short wardrobe. He recognized Paul's handwriting from across the room. Having rifled idly through some of his effects before, he knew both the look of the letters and the paper itself. Creeping over before Paul could notice he was moving, he glanced at the paper without picking it up.

I find myself wondering about that knife you took from

Sykes' body, and how clever it was to remember a detail like that. Though, I wish you had left it here with me, rather than thrown it out to sea—

Tom's eyebrows rose and he barely stopped himself from looking over his shoulder at Paul.

If I still had that awful thing, maybe I wouldn't half-believe I imagined our life together. Or you calling me your prize.

He blinked and found himself almost tearful, never mind who Sykes was and why Paul mentioned his body.

Then Paul's voice sluiced through the mournfulness.

"I've written to him," he said, lingering at Tom's right side. "More days than not. I started about a fortnight after they took him north. No, three weeks after." The words were soft, hesitant. They carried none of the anger Tom expected at an invasion of privacy.

In his mind, Tom saw piles of paper, stacks of notebooks. They'd all been here, undisturbed and strewn with dust, until Paul began cleaning his flat for the first time in years. He'd wanted to know what they were, if Paul was a clandestine novelist. Now he realized what they'd been. "All the papers you had up here..."

"It feels like I'm talking to him if I do it."

Looking around the tidy bedroom, Tom frowned. "Where did they go?"

"They're still here. Filed in the little office. I got them all in order and put them away." With the ghost of one of his more usual smirks, Paul said, "Theo wouldn't have seen them. I know you two were nosy, but I'm not that careless. If you could rifle through anything, it was left out because I didn't really care."

With a restrained snort, Tom disagreed gently. "You were livid when we said we learned where he was buried."

"I was startled. *That* made me angry."

Releasing a long breath, Tom said, "I'm still going with you."

3

I rritation wasn't Theo's usual state. Lennie knew enough of his character to understand ire was abnormal for him. They were sure it might always lurk under the surface when events warranted such negative reactions, but Theo rarely showed signs of vexation. Still, Theo muttered, uniquely agitated, "I should have gone with them. I'm not cut out for interacting with *everyone*." He sat with Lennie in the quiet and unoccupied kitchen: both of them were hiding after the morning they'd had.

A hint of irony lingered there, thought Lennie. By rights, a selkie should charm anybody. Theo generally did from what Lennie had seen, but that didn't stop life from littering his day with little pitfalls. It just meant people were kinder and generally more polite to Theo amidst all the tumult.

Mrs. Lloyd had an odious cold, Benson had caught it too and was not suffering quietly, and one of the present customers in an upstairs room exhibited signs of the same malady. It seemed to be making its rounds, as summer colds generally did. Meanwhile, the grocer had delivered another establishment's order—it wasn't the usual grocer that morning, but rather his son, who didn't seem to possess the same knack for running things smoothly.

Overall, the slightest of anyone's troubles at the moment was an irate ghost who couldn't follow his lover and was presently raising hell about it. From Lennie's perspective, Alastair was the least concerning problem. They couldn't sense him much themself, although David could and provided some insight into Alastair's state of mind. It was rather similar to the way an almanac might supply a circumspect bit of advice about the weather.

Almanacs were probably more immediately applicable, but Lennie loved David enough to let him prattle on about a ghost.

"Maybe you're too old to enjoy people, now." Lennie grinned at Theo, knowing through David that his looks and health obscured about a century of life. By design or otherwise, nobody but Theo knew his exact age.

"Hadn't even thought of it," said Theo. "Age really is the only thing that's changed since the last time I tried to do any work like this, and the last job I had was..." he appeared to consider his words with care. But Lennie didn't mind being reminded that Theo's last type of work was being David's paramour who was also ostensibly his secretary.

In the end, Theo didn't say it so much as acknowledge it with his pause. "Honestly, I didn't handle as many of David's peers and clients as you do. I just don't think I'm as suited to speaking to so many people throughout the day. Or night. You seem to like them. I just tolerated them."

They often liked people, although not always David's people.

Yes, three days into the Apollyons' absence, and

Theo already seemed at his limit for small inconveniences. Both Lennie and David had declared a short holiday and left Norwich for Cromer to come to his aid. The initial disquiet Lennie had felt in Theo's presence quickly ebbed into warm camaraderie.

Knowing he'd once been David's lover had roused envy and some apprehension. They felt they could not compete with an immaculately dressed selkie who was so well-spoken. There was the matter of their obvious social differences, too: Theo had alluded to attending university, and he clearly had money. Lennie knew from his clothes and hygiene that he did, and David also explained it was Theo who owned his and Tom's cottage.

Combined, it made Lennie a little nervous about their own background and whether David might one day decide they were too uncouth for him. Mostly, though, they were just jealous of Theo, not for his advantages but for his connection to David. Initially, they were jealous of Tom, too, and it actually felt a little worse: they and Tom were slightly more similar in class, so he felt like a more equivalent competitor.

Happily, these assessments had changed. It was clear that even if Theo and David could well be in each other's lives as long as both of them lived, a closed romantic relationship probably wasn't their best arrangement. The same was true of Tom and David, who were still prone to becoming rather terse with each other, especially if they were tired.

Despite any occasional sniping, there was a strong undercurrent of love that was both enjoyable and new to Lennie, and they weren't in a hurry to decide what it indicated. They knew people who had more than one lover, and in other situations, multiple lovers lived together. They felt, just as with most things chosen with a clear head, anything could work for anybody.

All the same, trying to imagine David, mostly, managing such a circumstance made them chuckle.

This was an excellent progression from being nebulously threatened by past lovers who were still underfoot. They'd rather laugh than be so insecure, as laughing was a more natural state for them.

A closeness had developed between Lennie and David's old lovers and friends, regardless of what it meant. It had to be said that whenever Robbie or Ralph were not involved in a situation, Lennie was actually prone to trusting. Not everyone knew it.

So even if there had been persistent thoughts of inadequacy when Lennie compared themself to Theo —or even Tom—they were largely gone. The choice to help Theo was an easy one. For the first time since Mum had died, Lennie felt they belonged to a family. Paul had helped them feel so, but it was a feeling that extended beyond him. Going to Theo when he was feeling overwhelmed just made sense.

Fortuitously, David's business contacts understood the quick announcement. They were all the sort of people who could venture to the sea on a whim. Although two had sent word of their displeasure at new delays to their orders or plans, nobody was in dire need of cloth or advice or any kind of merchandise. Lennie knew from keeping all the ledgers that David was operating at a profit, anyway, so in the event that either disengaged, it wouldn't matter much.

"It probably doesn't help that at night, they're expecting one of two short, brooding men with hazel eyes," said Lennie, referring to the Apollyons' appearances and Paul's regulars' expectations. "They remind me of cats, you know."

"The Apollyons?"

"Yes."

"Paul does, without a doubt. Tom... I'm not so sure." Theo tilted his head. "Though, perhaps a wildcat."

"You could always join them. Would it be quicker to swim your way there?"

"The train is more predictable. I did swim the last time, when I went to figure out where Alastair was buried. But back then, I needed to get out of my head a little bit."

Patiently, despite being eager to ask questions about what it was like—as a seal, did Theo think with human words, where did his clothes go when his body changed, did he feel the need to consume great quantities of fish—Lennie said, "That does make some sense."

He had gone after the span of time when David had almost, accidentally, captured him forever. Regardless of one's self-composure, and Theo evidenced a lot of that, such a circumstance had to be quite taxing. Some men went on benders, mused Lennie, while others who had the capacity became a seal for a few days.

"And if I went, who'd man The Shuck?"

"We would," said David's cultured voice, as he rounded the corner and came into the kitchen proper. As it always did, the tone made Lennie's flesh prickle agreeably. "I wondered if you'd both be here."

Lennie smiled, suspecting he would be of the same mind on the matter. "Exactly. We would. I was thinking we could stay behind and he could retrieve Paul and Tom."

"David Mills in trade?" Theo's eyes were warm and wicked.

"I'm already in trade, obviously, and an excellent trade we're doing, or we'd not be here for you. I can afford to take the time."

"Who knew I'd make a decent business manager?" Lennie said lightly, though they weren't too surprised that they both enjoyed and did well at it. There *were* those who sometimes peered at them when they spoke, because of their accent and its lack of refinement. But in the end, their aptitude and enthusiastic approach had usually won so far. If it did not, David either stepped in himself, or found a way to politely terminate the business arrangement before it went much deeper.

Ultimately, Lennie much preferred this line of work to what they'd done before, but on a day when people were being difficult, they comforted themself by imagining what it might be like to pickpocket sour Mr. Johnson or sanctimonious Mr. Hayes. They had imagined stealing from many of David's peers and clients.

"Still, in a pub? And the Apollyons' pub, at that?" Theo shook his head slowly, still openly teasing David in a kind fashion.

Lennie thought it was good for him.

"Luckily, my father isn't the ghost. I doubt I'll face any censure. The only ghost here is a former petty criminal who loves this place as much as he does its owner."

"And how *is* Alastair this morning?" Theo said. "Amused at all the activity and little mishaps, I'd hope. At least he can't catch a cold, and he doesn't need to eat. Actually, when I put it like that, being a ghost sounds terrible."

Balefully, Lennie eyed the kitchen's back door, wondering if the correct groceries would come at all.

While there was enough to manage for a day or two without issue, it would be best if they did arrive soon. Though, seeing as Mrs. Lloyd could not cook at present, they wondered who would cook anything that did manage to show up. They supposed they could manage a decent stew if pressed, but would prefer not to take on cooking duties if they didn't have to.

With a sigh, David shook his head and perched on the edge of the low, long table normally used to prepare meals. Answering Theo's question, he said, "He's staying in the flat. I think he's sulking. I don't blame him."

"Does he still want to go?" Theo asked the question Lennie would have.

"Yes, but it's more that he hates Paul went there if *he's* here."

Quiet fell between the three of them. It was a comfortable silence, if tired.

"All of this should stretch my belief, and it just doesn't," said Lennie.

Theo slipped them a slight, knowing, nod.

Lennie did ache on Paul's behalf, and for Alastair, whom they'd never even met. They gazed at David, who had calmed and come into his own so well in the last several weeks. The timid man who'd stunned their stepbrother with a touch was still there. But he was bolstered, tempered into the one who talked to a ghost as well as he did a chum, the one who took more on faith and was harder to rattle.

There'd been evidence of that faith the first Friday they'd gone to see Ralph on a *scheduled* visit—unlike when Lennie had slipped out of David's house under cover of night and paid an unplanned call. David, who despised Lennie's stepfather as well as their stepbrother, merely kissed them deeply before they left and murmured dinner would be waiting when they returned.

"Oh, Theo," said David. "This is as good a time as any to say, but if you go, or *when* you go, because I think you're going to... tell Paul to let himself have premonitions again."

Lennie was as perplexed as Theo looked.

"Tell him to what?" asked Theo. "How do you mean?

"We've a theory, Alastair and I, that he's just not having them? That he's stopped them, somehow. I haven't had a chance to ask Benson what he thinks, and I don't want to try now because I don't want to risk getting his cold." David glanced at Lennie. "And of course, I meant to talk to you. You would know better than us."

"Can he do that?" Theo looked at Lennie too. "Can you just make it all stop?"

Lennie thought of their ability to build barricades in their mind, which did help them focus and maintained others' privacy. It didn't seem exactly the same as halting everything to the fullest extent possible, but perhaps it meant the possibility of severing oneself from precognition also existed. "I expect we have our own ways of doing things. But I know I can stop myself from seeing scenes through another person. So if David had too much to drink and that's filtering through to me..."

They laughed a bit, drawing from experience to explain how it worked. "I can envision a wall, or bricks, or darkness. And then I stop seeing David, stop feeling David. I've never halted premonitions before, though."

They had never wanted to stop them, not even when Ralph was exploiting their talent.

"Sounds like it takes strength of character," Theo said.

"Why do you think Paul has stopped them altogether?" Lennie asked David.

"He told Benson he wasn't seeing anything at all. Alastair didn't think it was likely."

"Paul could be lying," said Lennie. They had only known Paul to lie by omission, but he seemed to be acting out of his usual character at present.

"It's just a sense," David said, and there was a note of apology in his voice. "But we think it's right."

Theo spoke quietly. "If he's turned his back on that, it's possible he's turned his back on sensing other things. I know he could feel me when I first came, but..."

"And he's said Benson and I feel similar," said David.

"I don't think anybody could eliminate every bit of preternatural sense they have," said Lennie. "But I think someone like Paul could damn well try, and he would likely get far."

There'd been enough evidence of Paul's obdurate nature for them to voice the opinion with confidence. In truth, though, Lennie must have been very fond of such a nature—David, as he eyed them, showed a glimpse of the same stubbornness. He, too, had managed to disavow part of himself until it was rather impossible to ignore. Lennie hoped Paul would not be driven to such extremes. But if what David and Alastair believed was correct, it seemed he already had been.

4

———

Portobello

So far, Tom had struggled with halting his consumption of alcohol due to the physical aspects of trying to stop. Every time he tried to cut back a little more, his body would protest even if his mind approved. His senses, too, already so heightened compared to many others', became keener. Whether it was because the alcohol was not present to influence him, or his abilities had rebounded in a strengthened state, he didn't know.

Months after his initial decision to give up drink, he hadn't suffered a serious relapse, other than one that Theo had demanded upon seeing he tried to wean himself too quickly. That, he could not quite count as his own choice, and it didn't cause him to fall headlong into the poor habits he'd once possessed.

Since then, he had settled for cutting back rather than eliminating, as utter strictness seemed to render his preternatural talents a little too keen for his taste.

It made him feel slightly weak, particularly when so much of the medical advice for those with his so-called affliction involved total abstinence.

But in the same way Dr. Jones could not have helped Paul before they came to Edinburgh, he could not advise Tom properly. If there were present-day medical men who integrated witchcraft and the unseen currents of the world with their practice, Tom had yet to meet them.

No longer was he going about his days in a fully intoxicated state, though, and that was an improvement by his measure. It was certainly more mindful, as well as richer.

But as Tom watched Paul approach Alastair's grave, he was closest to yearning for drunkenness than he'd been in ages. His fingers restlessly found the flask in his coat, and without taking his eyes away from Paul's slender form, he unscrewed the lid and took a drink. He'd purchased some whisky to keep on his person once they'd arrived at their inn. The small bottle sat in their room.

This was cognac Paul had wordlessly passed him the morning they'd left for the train north. Shadows had been under his eyes and he looked appropriately grim for a man who'd been drunk, then ill from his excess, for the first time in years. But he had been dressed and ready to depart.

Tom had carefully poured from the bottle itself into his smaller flask, acknowledging Paul's thoughtfulness with a nod.

Everyone knew Tom was still drinking medicinally except for Tom himself, who sometimes forgot until he was overstimulated by feelings, colors, and scents that did not belong to his own senses at all. He couldn't fully say if he was magically dependent in the same manner one could be physically dependent, but things did seem that way. At present, he'd decided not to fight it too much.

Blotting his mouth gently with the back of his sleeve, he kept his attention on Paul and let the intensity of the colors that surrounded him come to the fore. It had to have been the emotions Paul had been carrying and keeping to himself for so long, visible even from Tom's perch against a low tree branch. There wasn't much distance between them, not enough to blunt any of the greens or even render Paul fuzzy to the naked eye.

Just short of the foot of the grave, which they'd located with the help of an older man who appeared to be taking a constitutional in the cemetery, Paul abruptly turned on his heel and started back in Tom's direction.

The roiling, darkened shades emanating from him flared a little, glittering as sunlight on water, then Tom blinked them away. Standing, he waited for his uncle to approach and tried to keep his expression neutral, although he was nervous.

"All right?" Even as a rhetorical, regional phrase, one they were both incredibly used to hearing if not using—Paul was just well spoken, while Tom had learned to leave it aside because David, or David's father, had never liked it—the words smarted. A second after he asked it, Tom wished he could have asked anything else.

"No." For the first time since before Tom and Theo had come together, Paul sounded the way he had when Tom was a boy. One syllable was enough to demonstrate a decided shift from openness to tension.

Lightly, Tom tapped at his own temple. "Tell me what's going on in here."

Even as he seemed to draw himself inward, or try, Paul still appeared to struggle with an excess of feeling. In Tom's boyhood, Paul always seemed placid and exacting to a nephew whose peace was threatened regularly by whatever he happened to encounter. But Tom was now sure: he would never describe Paul as actually placid.

He'd thought several times since returning to Cromer that Paul had to be steeped in emotions. If nobody saw them, or only saw them manifested in taciturn behavior, that did not mean they were nonexistent. It just meant Paul was doing his best not to let them come to the fore.

"I can't," said Paul.

Feeling as though trying to draw him out again was better than ignoring his evident battle, Tom paused, then said, "That's all right. You don't have to. I just think it might help if you tried."

"No, I mean... I can't... I can't go to him. I can't look at that stone without wanting to gouge my eyes out."

The words sounded fairly mild for what they expressed. Though, a seer saying he wanted to gouge his eyes out did strike Tom as somewhat alarming. Several things competed to be said, and Tom decided not to say any. All of them were meant to allay a grief Tom knew he couldn't touch or alleviate. He finally decided on, "I think that's all right, too. He's not in the ground and we know it."

"No, *you* know it." With a smile jagged as a broken pint glass, Paul said, "*What* was the point of coming here?" His voice was, as ever, soft, although it might have been a little louder than normal. To a stranger, it would even be calm. Tom, however, knew better than to assume Paul maintained any calmness at present. "Why waste the time or spare the expense?"

At a loss, Tom said at length, "Because it matters." He glanced around the cemetery and sighed. It was a newer one, the old man had commented, before resettling his churchwarden between yellowed teeth.

Green and draped in daylight moderated by clouds, if such a mournful place might be called soothing, it would be this one. Tom felt Gran's grave was beautiful, too, but it was nearby a pub that was often raucous and the drifting noise could break one's contemplation. Father's, on the other hand, was much quieter but lacked any surrounding trees or foliage.

Alastair's resting place, not that he was strictly at rest, was as lovely as Paul and David said Alastair was himself; Tom couldn't make such a remark yet, having only been startled by brief glimpses of The Shuck's resident specter. Frankly, he didn't really wish to see him properly.

While Tom was biased and held little goodwill for Mr. Gow due to the strife he had caused Paul, even he could admit the place where Alastair was buried could have been much worse. An effort had been made to bury him somewhere meaningful, or at least where he'd lived with his wife and young son in Portobello. As Theo had ascertained, Alastair himself was born in Joppa.

Nonetheless, Tom still believed the choice to remove the body from Cromer, where Alastair had spent happy years, was a low blow. Certainly, refusing to reveal its final location was motivated by pettiness more than any true affection on Mr. Gow's part for his late adoptive father.

Paul removed his brown cap and nearly wrenched at his hair. "But it doesn't, Silence." Tom winced slightly. The use of his legal name never boded well in Paul's case. "It doesn't at all. It was childish to come. If he's anywhere, if any of you are to be believed, he's at home."

Tom let *if any of you are to be believed* pass without challenge. He knew Paul believed Benson, that he believed David and Lennie and Theo and himself. All the same, it was painful to see the patina of composure buffed away by such rough circumstances.

Paul's hand moved from his hair to scrub at his mouth. After Tom quietly offered him the flask, he took it without a protest or demure remark, and he drank deeply.

"I think we should rest," said Tom. "Have something to eat. You shouldn't pressure yourself."

He knew what desperation or feeling too much at once could drive one to do, and Paul might drive himself too hard for it to result in any healthy action. After all, Tom had not heavily ruminated upon ending his own life before choosing to try. He'd simply set out to do so. It *was* a choice, but at the time, the choice itself felt forced by the weight of accumulated difficulties and unrelenting perceptions.

When he met Paul's eyes, Tom saw something of himself, of who he had been and still could be if pushed. His own melancholy tended toward ink, and the ink occasionally did drench him still.

"Fine," said Paul.

"Perhaps this is enough."

"Turning away from him?" Paul's voice rose. "Again? How is *that* enough? Being so weak that I can't face a simple truth. People die."

"How have you turned away from him?" Tom could understand it in the sense of walking away from a grave, but *again* gave him pause for thought. Yet before Tom had a verbal answer, Paul's expression broke, and sobs said what he could or would not.

With a sigh, Tom stepped forward and embraced him, trying to keep him steady. Paul's collectedness had been false for the same number of years as it had existed, and Tom was man enough to understand such things now.

~

Upon his arrival to Portobello, Theo didn't know for certain where the Apollyons had chosen to stay. But one of the effects of cohabitating with Tom was a vague but persistent sense of what Tom could see: phantom colors, namely. In this instance, it was useful to pick up a mallard, or almost midnight blue, shade he associated in his mind's eye with Tom, which had mingled with a darker green that Theo assumed belonged to Paul.

Combined with the champagne and starlight lightness that only ever came to mind when he was near Tom, he knew it wouldn't be difficult to locate him. Pausing to consider the developing talent as he walked and followed the slight haze that drifted between buildings like smoke, Theo only *assumed* it was because of Tom and his abilities. He had little way of knowing for certain and only knew he was not going mad.

Or, he reasoned, since he was himself preternatural, perhaps it happened because a selkie was already receptive to such things. Although, maybe, as Theo always remembered whenever he came near to where he'd grown up, he was just malleable and too much of a mimic. His accent changed as soon as he came into contact with enough people from his prior home, an occurrence he hated but couldn't seem to help.

Even if he was picking up a small suggestion of what Tom could do, it might be because he was simply weak and lacked self-possession. He'd gone along with David for far too long, after all.

He didn't need to follow the mallard haze for an age: Tom rounded a corner within his line of sight and Theo went directly to him, winding his way past a number of men walking by. Though it had been just two nights since Tom and Paul had left Cromer, Theo was warmed upon seeing him.

He beamed at Tom's surprised expression, not un-aware of the pleasure and relief in his posture. "Thought you might miss me."

When he glimpsed Paul's tearstained face, Theo endeavored to look less pleased himself. Reflexively, he toyed with the golden chain at his neck, hidden under his shirt collar, and made sure the St. Julian medal faced front even though no one could see it.

"Always," said Tom. "But who is at The Shuck?"

"David."

The word made Tom look even more surprised, and Theo smiled a bit. "I know. But he was adamant, so I let him get on with it. Lennie is with him, too, so there *is* someone of the people to make sure King David doesn't get too highhanded."

Despite the joke, Theo felt it was possible David would prove to be an excellent interim landlord. The issue was how he might become overwhelmed in the process of doing something new, a type of overwhelm to which he seemed generally prone. But then again, managing relations with choosy clients, buyers, suppliers, and business associates had to have prepared David for some of the idiosyncrasies of working at a pub.

They might run out of Paul's ales and beers while things were in such flux, but everyone would simply have to live with it, should that occur.

Shaking his head more than nodding, Tom asked, "And how did you get here?" It was a tacit way of asking if he'd come as a seal, Theo knew. "Come on, we were just returning to our room. The pub over the road."

Wanting to ask what had transpired, but restraining his curiosity, Theo said, "Train." He brandished his bag slightly. "Wanted a change of clothes and all, and my pipe, seeing as I don't know how long we'll be here." It was unusual that Paul did not offer a dry remark in reply to the information that David was overseeing his public house, but Theo did not need to be told he was overwrought.

On a light chuckle, Tom said, "You know, you sound rather more Scot—"

"I know." Theo spoke up before Tom could go any further. "I don't need to be reminded. Think there's something wrong with me, or my ear, or my tongue." He softened the words with a chuckle.

"I like it."

As they walked, Paul still did not interject upon anything that Theo was sure he found amusing. At length, Theo said, "Well, I'm certain it will ease your way a little."

"Everyone has been hospitable already."

"Just wait. It's because you can pay them. But with me, it'll be different," he said only partially in jest.

Before they reached the building Tom was leading them to, an old man in a well-loved gray coat seemed to recognize Tom as he passed. He lingered and asked, "Did you find who you were looking for, sir? He *was* there, wasn't he?"

Tom, visibly tense to Theo's eye, said perfectly politely but with a twinge of nerves, "Seeing as he's dead, my friend, I do believe he was."

Theo did not miss the slight glance he gave his uncle, who was slightly gray-faced.

Seemingly quite a tolerant person, the old man touched the brim of his cap. "No disrespect meant, only I wondered who might have come from England to see Mr. Gow." Seeing the stony expression Tom bore, he halted himself. "Never mind. I *am* glad you found it."

Recovering, Tom managed to say, "Thank you."

The man walked on, leaving snarled curiosity and bewilderment in his wake. Theo was curious, anyway, and Tom appeared bewildered once the man's back was turned.

But it was Paul whom Theo worried for: the tension in his shoulders, the tautness in his red-nosed, otherwise pale face, were telltale signs of a man very close to the brink. The brink of what, precisely, would remain to be seen. When in crisis, Paul was not normally the sort to drink and make sudden plans, yet there were apparently some things that would induce him to do so.

Unfortunately for the Apollyons, Theo knew they rarely did anything by half.

5

———

Cromer

David probably wouldn't be able to kill Ralph this week.

Or next week.

He would send some word to Robbie that he was here, keeping The Shuck running. He was in neither of his so-called fancy homes. Robbie had been to both, one once, the other twice for dinner. The dinners in Cromer had been more awkward affairs than Robbie's breaking and entering in Norwich. But Lennie was trying to show their sibling that life did not have to be comprised entirely of caring for an addled, raving, awful father or committing larceny and other crimes to pay for said father's upkeep.

In truth, David admired their optimism. Personally, he did not think Robbie capable of becoming other than what he was.

He looked up at Paul's ceiling, lying on his back in Paul's bed, hearing the tick of Paul's clock on the mantel. It was strange to be in such an intimate place belonging to man who, until very recently, held little discernible high regard for him. But last month it had all changed, and things were still in transition. What a thing to be thinking, treating murder like an item on a list of things he needed to do.

Then he blinked, always nervous he might think such a thing and Lennie would come to know it. They had no soft feelings for their stepfather, but still, they would probably not condone him being murdered and certainly would not approve of David doing it.

If they even believe I could.

Ironically, perhaps, since his contemplation of murder was for them. Ralph was a threat to Lennie's happiness and safety, and David felt such a fury whenever he thought of how abominably Lennie had been treated that it could only be called murderous.

Alastair said he believed David could, but it was more the belief of an eager parent in a child attempting a mildly difficult recitation. Not entirely real, but nicely feigned. Alastair *had* heard him threaten Robbie in a cellar. Because David disliked Robbie and had once knocked him flat with a brief touch, it hadn't been hard to threaten.

Anyway, the touch had been laced with some kind of magic he still did not know how to command. It felt allied with his ability to sense ghosts, but he could not say more than that.

He yawned, waiting for Lennie to join him in the bed, trying to think less of murder and more of how absolutely mad running this public house was. Paul had been born to it and done nothing else, so he made it look efficient, but David had learned it took considerable skill. He could not say it that way, knew he shouldn't. But he meant it as a compliment and not a slight.

Glancing at the bedroom's doorway, he knew Alastair was in the parlor beyond, listening to Lennie chatter about this and that. Ghosts didn't need to sleep, but David had offered him this room for his own use, whatever the use was. Alastair had shrugged and said he'd rather go through Paul's notes to him.

Lennie, the darling that they were, was patiently setting out the notes, letters, so Alastair could peruse as many of them as possible. It was sweet and conciliatory, meant to assuage him. He'd wanted to go with Paul, indubitably, but whenever he tried to step out of the taproom, he said *something* yanked him back. This was, Alastair groused, almost as infuriating as only having the mild suggestion of his senses and little ability to interact with anything physical.

It was beyond anyone's experiences, including Benson's, though he seemed older than dirt itself. David was always mildly surprised when he didn't have answers due to how worldly he seemed. Since Alastair's senses did seem to be expanding gradually, David was of a mind that at some point, he might well be able to move things on his own.

Or smell Paul's hair.

It was something Alastair lamented about within that first few days of being able to communicate. He could see it and be so close to it, yet not smell it. Imagining such a predicament verged on imagining hell, or maybe purgatory, so David tried not to imagine what it actually would feel like to be separated from Lennie in the same way.

David froze as another idea entered his mind. It could be a thought born of Gothic novels and some of Benson's gruff hints, but he wondered how easily Alastair could truly possess him.

If so, he'd be able to take a train and follow Paul anywhere, dragging David behind him like a kite. He glanced at his hands on top of the bedclothes. He'd hope in such a scenario that Alastair wouldn't feel the need to seek or give himself tattoos for old times' sake.

As strongly as the thought came, David endeavored to ignore it. He could barely contemplate the realities of sharing The Shuck with a dead man, and here he was doing it.

At least the dead man in question was courteous, never mind whatever he'd been in life. Alastair probably wouldn't *want* to tow David about like a kite. However, David was finding that the seemingly intrusive thoughts in his head had an irksome way of being right.

"I think I've given him enough reading material to last all night." Lennie strode through the doorway so lightly that the old floorboards didn't so much as shift. "Anyway, we'll be up so early that I can set out new things even if he does manage to peruse all of that." With a glance over their shoulder, they closed the bedroom door. "It's strange, talking to air. But then I think he reckoned that if he just stood in front of the old mirror above the mantel... I could at least see him."

Pulling himself up so he could sit against the headboard, David said, "I read somewhere that some people use mirrors for scrying because they can reflect the dead."

Always one to read as a child, then having lost the habit of reading books he actually enjoyed as a young man at university, David had rediscovered his love of reading around the same time he met Lennie. Part of it had been in the name of research, for he had been thrust into a world full of things he'd either disavowed or never discovered. But it was revelatory to read for pleasure even if it served a purpose. There was also a slight thrill to reading things Father would have disapproved of, which was almost anything. But especially things of an occult nature.

As he thought back to the prior December, he recalled Theo making some comment about his father's ghost. At the time, David was in no position to have seen or sensed anything of the sort, and even now during his nights in the Mills' house in Cromer, he felt nothing out of the ordinary. It followed that Mr. Mills, Senior, was not lingering as some ghastly or displeased shade, which was a blessing overall.

If Father hadn't liked Theo, which he hadn't—as much as he was capable of disliking somebody in such a state of mental confusion—he would not like Lennie.

David had thought before that ghosts might be as they were when they'd become such creatures. Coming to know Alastair bolstered his initial idea. In the end, if Father were a ghost and David simply was unable to see him, he might have little idea what was going on around him because he had been locked in a backward-looking haze before he died. He'd been prone to describing something that had happened when he was the age of twenty, not bursts of anger or paranoia.

Unlike Ralph, according to Robbie.

Alastair was the man he'd been just prior to his death, something Benson could confirm even if Paul couldn't. Cheerful, pragmatic, prone to cursing, almost painfully devoted to Paul. Surprisingly keen on David's clandestine plans with Robbie, or at least the shadowy, only partially manifested version of him had been. It made sense when one took into account Alastair's prior ties to illicit activities, although David was uncertain if Alastair had ever killed anyone despite his outwardly menacing demeanor.

Not that they'd discussed David's wish to kill Ralph overmuch. Alastair obviously had more on his mind, but David kept waiting for it to come up, anxious his own half of the conversation might be overheard. He supposed it would be.

"Suppose that follows," said Lennie, undressing and folding their clothes to hang over the small valet in the corner. "Mum saw things in her looking glass, and aren't there all sorts of stories about scrying in mirrors and water and silver?"

Eying them as they spoke, thinking little about scrying and more about the span of skin between their shoulders, David added, "And crystal balls."

"Anyway, if Alastair stands still in view of that mirror, I can make eye contact and all. He waved at me. Didn't try to talk, which is good, because I can't read lips. And I can't hear him."

"No, he wasn't talking. I could have heard him from in here. Maybe he's just sick of speaking to everyone but Paul."

Naked, now, all clothes properly laid aside, Lennie went to the basin of clean water and quickly washed their face. David smiled at their back, knowing they enjoyed walking about without clothing as much as they enjoyed teasing him.

"I'm glad I thought of it. Taking more of them out so he can read." They dried their face. "Makes the most sense to do it up here, anyway. Wouldn't think Paul wants them where customers can see them."

"And it'd look terribly disorderly. Bits of paper on every surface." David shifted over so that Lennie could come and rest alongside him, then covered them both again with the linen sheets. He usually slept wearing something, the result of a very prim childhood, but

Lennie was prone to sleeping in the nude. "You don't think he'll barge in here?"

"You're the person speaking to him the most." Lennie slipped a hand around David's waist and stroked at him through his shirt. "You tell me."

"If I were him, I couldn't tear myself away from those notes. I don't need to talk to him to know. I just... sometimes, it's difficult to remember I set my own standards now and at least in private, I don't need to conform or worry much about decency."

"You really aren't as proper as you say."

David chuckled and smiled down at Lennie. "At any rate, if he does come in, you won't even notice. I will, but you'll be fine."

"Hadn't thought of that," said Lennie. They yawned. "Good night. Love you. You'd best wake me early or you'll drown in tasks."

As he watched Lennie's eyes fall closed, David thought he would do just about anything to protect this kind of peace. It might be relatively new, only a fledgling compared to others' relationships. But he wanted to ensure it would last for both his and Lennie's sake.

Even if it could not last every second, he wanted to foster circumstances in which their lives were permeated by warmth and the capacity for love. He didn't want the future to be riddled with the possibility of bitter, hypocritical old men wreaking havoc.

6

———

Portobello

In a cheerful, well attended pub far from either of the ones he'd known since childhood, Tom watched his uncle break the day after their visit to the cemetery.

Time finally won out against Paul's remarkable force of will. It left him huddled in a wooden chair in an unobtrusive corner as he wept. This show of supposed male weakness didn't seem to rouse the concern or discomfort of the locals, who milled about in a late afternoon throng. The throng seemed used to men crying.

Tom didn't know if whisky would be helpful, but he handed some over all the same, the little glass cool in his hand.

Paul took it, but didn't drink yet. Instead, he inhaled and seemed to gather his senses enough to remark, "This really is poor form, drinking so much around you."

"It's nothing," said Tom. Truly, it mattered little to him if anyone abstained or did not. He knew being around spirits could pose a problem for some who were trying to give them up. Thankfully, it wasn't one of his own issues, or at the least, it did not tempt him too much. He supposed he was accustomed to it because he'd grown up around alcohol, seeing as his father, uncle, and mother all kept public houses. He regarded Paul with what he hoped was a level expression that did not display too much worry. "Do you want to talk, now?"

While pressing his uncle usually ended in little but obdurate silence, he felt it was good now to keep asking questions. The worst Paul could do was dismiss him, and they'd had years of practice at that.

Theo returned from the bar with a loosely wrapped sandwich, which he sat on the table between Paul and Tom. "She wouldn't take my money."

It was hard to tell if he was pleased or resigned.

"Because you're Scottish or you're a selkie?" Paul said, and Tom was glad to see a glimmer of his normal humor.

Theo's smile was small and genuine. "Both, at a guess. I can't abandon either of them. And sometimes, the way you people go on about it, you'd think being a seal some of the time makes me a siren. Ridiculous, really. Seals are nothing like mermaids. They did inspire some of the mermaid legends, though, you know."

When Paul took part of the sandwich and nibbled before sipping his whisky, Theo's smile grew as he settled on the bench next to Tom. Under cover of the table, Tom slid a hand atop his thigh. A raucous man called to his friend at a table opposite the three of them, and Tom followed his progress as he wound through the gaggle.

Intoxicated people often provided the biggest preternatural distractions, even now. In this man's case, he threw out shocking orange ripples that reached his friend well before he actually did. *Never did like orange.* Tom retrained his eyes upon Paul, who ate, if not eagerly, then readily.

At length, Paul said, "I haven't had a premonition in years."

First, Tom thought he'd misheard. "You what?"

Theo's grave eyes, which Tom caught when he slipped a glance to his left, said he had not misheard. But he pressed on. "Of course you have. You... told me they were like spiderwebs. That it was like being in a web."

"Well, I didn't lie about that."

Then again, Paul had never actively lied about anything. His method of choice was lying by omission. It *had* taken Tom reaching adulthood to discover he wasn't the only person in his family with a preternatural inclination. But the last time they'd really spoken of Paul's abilities and their genesis, Tom hadn't thought to ask about minute details. He'd been preoccupied by Theo and David, and with discovering Paul was a seer. They hadn't even used that word, seer.

Tom took the second half of the sandwich for himself, more to have something to do. "You only ever lied by withholding things."

"And some might not consider that lying at all," said Theo.

Tom gently squeezed his thigh with his unoccupied hand, acknowledging Theo might have different views on the matter of disclosing or not disclosing certain details. That had been a matter of self-preservation for him, and a matter that Tom did not question excessively. He did not need to be given Theo's skin to feel close to him.

"I did tell you I thought it was a curse when Alastair died," said Paul, tilting his head slightly as he considered a candle on a tabletop two away from theirs. Then his gaze alighted on their own stubby candle. The afternoon was dreary, so daylight did not illuminate much on its own. "And for a while, I truly believed it was. Why show me so much over the years, and not that?" He blinked and looked at Tom again.

It was Theo who seemed to understand the implications first. He shifted slightly in his seat next to Tom, and said, "You wanted it to go away, so you started not to look when the visions came calling."

Tom tried to comfort himself by recalling Theo was older and generally quicker at gleaning motivations behind others' behavior.

In a way, Tom was envious of Paul's determination. He'd never been able to consistently look away from anything he saw or felt, not until recently in his life, and that inability, along with a deep sense of alienation from others because of what he could see, led him down thorny paths. It had taken the love of those around him, as well as a commitment to his own survival, to gain some semblance of order and calm within his mind.

He couldn't imagine simply *not looking* if a loud, drunk stranger cast tendrils of orange in his view, or when Toothless Rob, one of his uncle's regular patrons at The Shuck, left such an expansive feeling of melancholy in the taproom. After he'd eventually learned Rob had lost his family in a house fire, the melancholy made sense, as did the constant drunkenness and home brewing.

But knowing its source made Tom no more able to rationalize or ignore its presence.

Setting down the bite he'd had yet to eat and

chasing the sandwich with whisky, Paul nodded. "It was difficult at first, but it got easier with practice."

"Is it that you haven't had one in years?" Theo said. In a less refined person, his tone could be called shrewd, but somehow he made it sound more inquisitive. Interested in the person rather than the choice, felt Tom, which made him more likely to receive answers. "Or is it that you've ignored them for years?"

Sighing before he replied, Paul said, "Remind me never to *actually* lie to you. They've become far less sharp, far less immersive. It's... the same as trying to see through heavy rain." He rubbed at both of his temples with his pointer fingers. "I suppose that's close enough to ignoring them."

Tom sat back and recalled his own sense of Paul's roiling shame when they'd had their first man-to-man talk on the subject, tucked away in his flat that was then more like a mausoleum, surrounded by all the papers that did turn out to have a purpose. It hadn't been clear then that Paul was evading him, largely because he was suppling a shocking enough revelation without there being more to the proceedings. Tom didn't think there could be anything beyond his uncle being a seer.

But his uncle was a *lapsed* seer. The evasion was so subtle, so without an ulterior motive to harm, that Tom hadn't noticed it. Paul had so adroitly shifted the conversation to him, to his nephew.

Tom studied him. "Did you want to tell me, back when we spoke—after you and Benson said Theo had left his skin behind in Cromer?" It felt like a lifetime ago.

"I felt guilty over the fact we were only speaking just then as equals," said Paul. He drained his glass. "That I'd pushed you away for years." He smiled, the lines around his mouth deepening. "I must confess, I wanted you to feel less alone before I ventured to tell you I wasn't *really* using my abilities."

Tom looked to Theo for some sign as to what to say or do. Ever gentle, Theo gave him the slyest and most minute of winks, then said to Paul, "No, well, you're always a witch, or a seer, aren't you? That's the trouble." He cleared his throat. "You did what David did."

"I *am* about as tightly wound as he is," said Paul, and Tom bit down a smirk at his dourness. "Wasn't always, though."

"Can't have been." Theo smirked. "You were with someone like Alastair."

"He's with someone like Lennie. David, I mean," Tom said. His eyebrows arched. "And before that, he was with me. Then some oily Cambridge boys up to no good. And Theo. So how tightly wound can he actually be? Apologies, Paul, but you may win on that front, given all your experience in self-denial."

Paul's earnest, almost bashful grin given in reply to the teasing was the best reward he could have received.

"That's exactly what it is," said Theo. "Paul, maybe it's time to just... let go. Let it come back. I don't think you're protecting yourself, now. It might be harming you more than anything."

"Not that I think you need to go find yourself a toff in the name of distraction, but I agree," said Tom, eying Paul's expression as it flickered. He would need to ask Theo, once they were alone, if the topic of this conversation was why he had left The Shuck in David's hands to come here. Though Theo's approach was coaxing and soft, he retained a seriousness that belied more concern than he outwardly conveyed.

It had never been a habit of Tom's to push anyone to divulge more than they wanted, if only because he was so busy managing his own thoughts and sensitivities that he could hardly deal with anyone's verbal confessions. He wished it was possible to divine Paul's reasoning without asking for it.

Already, he had—quite cautiously so as to avoid a deluge—let some of his guard down as Paul spoke. Perhaps it was easier to feel what Paul felt because they were on good terms now. They had been since last December. Paul was no longer avoiding Tom out of a misguided sense of protectiveness.

Dismay, fear, longing, regret, and for the first time, hope's slow bleed all radiated from Paul. Tom smiled. The tentative emergence of hope made him believe Paul could surface from this in relatively good stead.

The raucous man who'd dripped orange everywhere shouted something, louder than the rest of the milling throng, and certainly louder than the friend whom he'd joined. Focused as he was on Paul, Tom didn't care to know what it was.

As he straightened his hat, Theo's dark eyes lingered on the man. "Someone's had too much to drink."

"I don't know if I can let go," said Paul quietly. "Rather, it scares me to think of it."

"That's normal. It isn't easy to relinquish our old self," said Theo. His voice held nothing but kindness. "But you're not even in control, like this, are you? Not if... fear, or... bitterness... is dictating so much of your life."

"I had thought, before I left to come here..."

"Before you got so pissed that you purchased *tickets to Scotland* without telling anyone until after you'd done it?" Tom said, half-smiling at Paul in spite of raising his voice slightly. "What did you think we'd do? Stop you? No, we'd come along."

"If that's the worst thing I've done in fifteen years, it isn't terrible. Before I got so pissed that I decided to finally come here, yes, I..." Paul's voice trailed off, and after a slight pause, he said, "I started to wonder if I was the one keeping Alastair from, well, myself."

This admission, Tom noticed, caused relief to play across Theo's fine features.

Theo leaned just across the table as though for emphasis. Tom took his hand from his thigh as he moved toward Paul. "That is exactly why I—"

But Theo was interrupted by a dry voice. "So *good* to see the man my father chose over me. It's been years."

7

───────

Theo looked at the speaker, a man with dull, pewter-threaded golden hair and sea-glass green eyes. Before saying a word, he first glanced away and gauged Paul's expression.

Paul stared at the newcomer as though stymied by a collision of contradictory thoughts. It might've been the whisky slowing him down. But even when he was inebriated, Paul's mind seemed quick; Theo had little doubt he was thinking more than his silence said.

Judging by the words, the speaker's snide tone, and Paul's reaction, this was very likely James Gow, Alastair's son by marriage.

If it was, Theo wondered if he should usher the Apollyons and Mr. Gow outside. He had a sense the discussion could turn into a row. Not because of Paul, who actually looked like he might never move again, but because of the simmering fury under Mr. Gow's restrained expression. His body was coiled and tense under reasonably well tailored clothes in shades of brown. They were nondescript and a couple of years old, but quality made.

"Thank you, Ives," said Mr. Gow, looking to the loud drunk man. "These were the ones Steven said he spoke to yesterday?" Seeming to receive an affirmative in the form of a nod rather than more slurred shouting, because Theo could neither see Ives nor hear a reply, Mr. Gow smirked and said as though to no one, "Who knew Steven's wee constitutionals would amount to anything?" His eyes fell upon Paul again, and they weren't at all welcoming.

Huffing, Theo surmised the drunk might have been shouting about *them* to Mr. Gow as Mr. Gow entered. Their backs were to the door and the gaggle of people obscured those who entered the pub.

It seemed Tom had similar thoughts, for he said after a tense moment of quiet, "Sometimes I forget Cromer isn't the only place where *everyone* knows everyone." He looked up at Mr. Gow, who stood stiffly with the busy taproom as his backdrop.

Theo would wager good money that all within were trying to listen, despite the volume of ambient noise changing little, and the incoming sounds of conveyances and pedestrians from outside.

Continuing with the slightest of sneers, Tom said, "But you do have the advantage of me."

"His kind don't stand on ceremony," said Mr. Gow. He sat in the chair next to Paul's.

"What kind?" Tom's voice was light, inquiring, but Theo knew better than to assume Tom was calm. Had he any interest in warning Mr. Gow, Theo might tell him to tread carefully.

"You must be a son," Mr. Gow said. His gaze swept across Tom as though taking in a painting he didn't particularly enjoy.

"Nephew," said Tom, with a terse shake of his head. "Also Mr. Apollyon." Then, possibly because his Tom could never resist being a bit contrary, he added,

"From what I've heard, you don't take after your father at all. Funny, that."

For a brief moment, Theo closed his eyes, wishing he could signal Tom not to test Mr. Gow so overtly. When he opened them again, Tom seemed to be spoiling for a fight. Mr. Gow's upper lip had curled into an unpleasant smile.

"My family was not terribly conventional," said Mr. Gow.

"Neither is mine," Tom said.

Apparently deciding Tom was not worth the same effort as Paul, Mr. Gow redirected his attention to the elder Apollyon. "You still don't look like much. But then, there is no accounting for taste."

Most of what Theo knew about Paul's past had come while he was poring over receipts and ledgers, with Paul sometimes glancing over his shoulder and offering a remark or two. He understood Paul and Mr. Gow met when he came to Cromer after Alastair died. As they all knew, Mr. Gow demanded his father be brought north.

To his credit, Paul had tried to explain a situation that couldn't have been easy for Mr. Gow, but was also incredibly complex for Alastair. It was to no avail: Mr. Gow cared to understand none of it. He was understandably furious, although Theo could never quite justify what had been done to Paul. He could see what merited Mr. Gow's secretive retaliation, but now considered Paul family and the impact upon him had been almost absolute.

Everyone's potential pain was obvious to Theo—a son, the product of a long, loving liaison between his parents, Arthur and Evie. Ultimately left behind by the father who'd raised him.

Evidently, Evie and Alastair had been bosom

friends. Alastair was more than willing to bring up another man's child in his house, and Arthur was more than good to Evie and reputedly good-natured to most everyone.

The potential disgrace of their neighbors and peers knowing the truth of their situation, though most already seemed to understand it, was simpler to bear than a separation, according to Evie's opinion. It seemed the two men in her life had been willing to let her set the course in that regard, and also that nobody in the vicinity cared much about the situation in reality.

After a surreptitious glance at Mr. Gow, Theo decided he probably hadn't inherited Arthur's good nature. Or Evie's. It was equally possible that he'd never let himself cultivate one, or this was just not the moment to see the best in him.

Though Paul had not said, Theo suspected Alastair entered marriage already knowing he was an unspeakable, and not the sort of man who was built for a staid and normal life. A wife, children, an occupation. Everything Theo knew of Alastair spoke to a possession of loyalty, but it also told him Alastair would not have been content with the normal order of things. Theo sympathized.

By his own nature, he was incapable of such things and remained excluded from attaining that kind of respectability.

Finding his voice, Paul said, "James." It didn't seem to Theo that Paul was being pointedly casual with his use of the Christian name. He just sounded rather shocked. "You have quite the bevy of friends, if they all alert you so quickly to an undesirable's presence."

Mr. Gow waved a hand as though it was of no import what sort of friends he had or how many of them there were. "It's as your nephew says. We know each other, and most everyone knew my father left me as soon as I had the smallest chance of fending for myself. It just confirmed what they already knew, really, that he wasn't my father at all. It's all right. Arthur stepped in. He was the grandfather my children knew."

Theo wasn't fooled by the offhanded air. This wasn't the hurt carried by a man who *hated* the father he'd known. Unless he missed his guess, Mr. Gow was more angry that Alastair had abandoned him and less angry that he was born out of wedlock. For the latter, at least, Theo was grateful. But he still felt Mr. Gow would not be above suggesting the perverse for his own amusement. He seemed jealous of Paul for capturing his father's attention, and appeared interested in needling and causing dismay.

Why else, thought Theo, would he chance making a scene like this one?

It was, in short, pettiness. Perhaps a sort of infantile viciousness. He wasn't really making true pronouncements on anyone's moral state, whatever he said about *his kind.*

Not that Paul seemed to see it, or Theo would expect him to be the bigger man. No one won in this situation.

"When *did* you know?" Paul asked, his words barely carrying over the pub's collective, yet still rather hushed noise. "About Evie—I mean to say, your mother—and Arthur? Alastair..." he caught himself when he spied Mr. Gow's disapproving face. "When I first met your father, I don't think you did."

At that, Theo realized Paul and Mr. Gow must not have discussed this particular point some years ago. Well, when there was a body to be moved, and in Mr.

Gow's case, a bitter point to be made, there might not have been a spare moment to ask about family secrets.

A flash of ire passed through Mr. Gow's demeanor, then it vanished. But his speech was clipped to reflect it. "He finally told me. Alastair. In a letter. After he left. Said he *disagreed with my mother*, who apparently never wanted to tell me at all. How she thought I wouldn't find out, I don't know. But she was a silly thing."

Paul kept his face admirably serene. When Theo looked at Tom, Tom's expression mirrored the same forced peacefulness.

Mr. Gow snorted when neither of them interjected. "She must have been quite silly, to live the life she did."

Not for the first time in recent years, Theo felt his age acutely. Little besides cruelty could make him pass quick judgement. It wasn't his business to judge a woman who'd married, but later fell in love with somebody else. If her husband would never love her as he could a man, Theo could not blame her.

Anyway, social expectations were such that women were derided for being old maids. Women without means might also be expected to marry as soon as they could to avoid being burdens upon their parents.

How young were Evie and Alastair when they married? Theo kept the question to himself. Perhaps it was a marriage of convenience, in a sense.

"Why have you sought us out?" Tom was decidedly frosty, skipping past polite deference or apologies to get straight to the point. Theo loved his protectiveness.

"I don't care what *you* do. Prowl wherever you'd like," said Mr. Gow. "I've only sought *him* out." He fixed his eyes on Paul. "He needs to leave."

"Very well, then, *Mr. Gow*," Tom said. "How *exactly* did you come to know we were here? I gather it had something to do with the charming Ives over there. Or Steven, whoever that is."

"Word travels fast, and nobody visits that grave. Arthur is buried with my mother; Alastair is alone."

Remaining silent, Theo wondered where Arthur and Evie were buried and reckoned the bitterest of men still had hearts despite their hard words.

Perhaps Paul was trying to adjust to the conversation at hand, but instead of voicing any pain at his lover being left alone, he just started to ask another question. "You never wrote him. What *did* you do when he—"

One that, from Theo's view, seemed blissfully unaware of Mr. Gow's evident, tightly laced anger.

It was a mistake. Theo knew before Paul did. This was no warm acquaintance and there would very likely be no reconciliation at all. Recoiling slightly, Mr. Gow shook his head. "When I was left with a letter and a pile of banknotes one evening? When I expected my father and tea?"

"He'd said—"

Mr. Gow struck the table that separated him and Paul, interrupting Paul's rather feeble words. He relaxed his clenched fist before he spoke. "Hang what he said. Do you know what *else* he said in his first letter? That he was certain he would come back. That he would make sure I was getting on. So I waited."

Meanwhile, Tom remained as coiled as Theo had ever seen him.

Paul winced, a small expression. But to anyone who knew him, it spoke volumes.

"Next thing I heard from him, he'd taken work

with you. He didn't say anything about coming back, not in that letter, not in the next one."

"I've already tried to tell you," said Paul, his face ashen. "I told you years ago. He never wanted you to lack anything. He *wanted* to make sure you were all right. He would have come to you if you'd asked."

"I shouldn't have had to ask." With that, Mr. Gow rose from his seat. Any pretense that the rest of the pub was not trying to hear the conversation vanished, and Theo cringed at this new almost-silence.

Some of Paul's customary backbone seemed to reappear then. He said, "You weren't a child. He didn't leave you to die." Whether Theo agreed with Paul's defense of Alastair, or Mr. Gow's anger, he couldn't decide. He saw the genesis and impact of both. Continuing, Paul said, "*Your father* felt guilty. Not that he said a bad word about you, or your mother, or Arthur. He didn't *say* much at all."

"I don't know why he left. I don't care who the hell he buggered," Mr. Gow said, as dismissive as one might be when discussing the dreich weather.

But it was still the thing that brought Paul to his feet. His spindly chair wobbled in its corner.

Seeming to understand his words' power, Mr. Gow added, probably sensing a weakness, "He had men before you, you know. So *you* must have done something he *really* liked."

It wasn't entirely possible to tell if Mr. Gow lied or spoke the truth, but it didn't matter.

Theo rose carefully, exchanging a glance with Tom, who looked like he wished to intervene and send Mr. Gow home in a cart. Gingerly, Theo went around the small table and stopped at its head, and murmured, "Gentleman, might we take this outdoors?" Normally, when he spoke cajolingly to men, it worked.

This time, it did not.

Both Mr. Gow and Paul ignored him, so he moved to place himself between them. Not entirely, but enough so that his body was partially angled between theirs. He rested his palm on the tabletop, mindful of the candle, and tried again. "Mr. Gow, we've no quarrel with you."

"Tell me, Mr. Apollyon—did you promise him everything?" Theo thought Mr. Gow's question a strange one, until it turned into a clear attempt to bait Paul. "I heard him, just once, with one of his lovers in our house," Mr. Gow continued.

"Paul," Tom said, a warning in the one word.

Because he faced Mr. Gow, Theo couldn't see what Paul was doing. He imagined it merited some concern. If Tom, of all men, sounded cautionary, Paul must look as though he wanted to commit a murder.

"He was ever so good about keeping that part of his life private, except for that *one* time. He didn't realize I'd returned home from school so quickly that day. Mother was out." Mr. Gow chuckled without mirth. "I didn't *see* a thing. I stopped myself outside."

Theo flinched minutely, guessing what might come next.

"But I *heard* how his paramour moaned he'd give him everything." Then Mr. Gow paused for effect, not that any of them present needed to consider the situation at which he hinted. "Really, anyone on the street might've heard. And I suspect many of us have overheard our parents. Why should it bother me if it was a man?"

With rather frightening speed, Theo felt himself yanked out of the way, and Paul landed a sharp, quick right on Mr. Gow's smug face.

Startled and cast off-balance, Theo flailed about a

little, hissing when his palm met the candle's flame as he groped for purchase. He didn't draw it back quickly enough to avoid a burn, but when he glanced down, the damage was not so severe. His skin was flushed red but there was no blistering yet. If a blister appeared, he felt it would be minor. As an apothecary, his father had treated many similar burns.

Thank goodness for small favors. It would heal fairly quickly, he knew, an advantage to being a selkie. Unless his skin was taken from him, he would recover from minor things more efficiently than somebody who was not.

The hand on his coat, clutching the fabric between his shoulders, relinquished him. Paul mumbled, "Fuck."

Mr. Gow rubbed at the side of his face as the gaggle of pub-goers murmured ominously. "Christ alive, man."

Paul said from behind Theo, "I wouldn't have let you fall, Theo." He did not address Mr. Gow's blaspheming.

"Next time," said Theo, managing a smile, "a simple 'duck' will suffice." He was still catching his breath when Tom stood at last.

"Enough." Tom's tone brooked no argument. Under other circumstances, Theo would have found the steel in his voice titillating. "Mr. Gow, I expect that bruise on your cheek will fade within the week. We'll leave you, and you can forget we ever came." He hardly looked at Paul, but said in a gentler voice likely meant for him, "We'll catch a morning train."

Nodding, Theo wondered if they might need to find new lodgings, seeing as they would otherwise retire to rooms directly above where Paul had struck a local. Nobody knew he was normally quite a mild, quiet man.

From the way she was presently glaring at them, Theo surmised the barkeep regretted giving up a sandwich for nothing.

8

Cromer

The streets were quiet as morning dawned, bringing with it familiarly dull, summer sunlight veiled in clouds. Despite the peace, David hadn't slept at all.

He shifted his eyes to spy Lennie, dead to the world under cover of soft linen and cotton. They rarely slept poorly, a skill he envied. Even a peevish ghost didn't have the power to rouse them, it seemed. His eyelids heavy, he sat up in bed. If he had not slept, there was a chance some of the customers hadn't.

The Shuck always seemed larger than it actually was, and at present they had three guests, besides Benson and two regular tenants. Still, it wouldn't do for anyone paying to reside here to be disturbed. He took a moment and hauled himself up, unaware if the oppression pressing on him like the start of a storm, or the scuffling noises, were realities others could feel. It almost seemed as though he could, if he strained his ears, hear a distant howl of pain or sorrow. But it was incredibly faint, just enough to make him question if it existed.

Nonetheless, he had an idea of where or who it all radiated from. "Alastair?"

He crept into the main room in Paul's flat, still littered with the papers Lennie had set out the night before. The light was weak, dreamlike, casting the space in shadows and pewter. Looking about, he saw Alastair with his back turned to him, looking out the window that allowed for a view of the sea beyond the promenade.

Joining him, David watched the capricious water, gray or deep green one moment, then churning with white the next. He didn't know what to say, so it seemed best to say nothing. Keeping his emotions and thoughts purely to himself was a more habitual thing than speaking overmuch to those around him anyway. Though it was liberating to speak his mind, it could also be exhausting.

He simply hadn't had enough practice. When silence fell over him, it was calming and familiar.

Then Alastair spoke. "I'm sorry."

"For what?"

"Waking you up. I suppose you can hear me shuffling through the papers and pacing about?"

David waved his hand, a dismissive gesture. Upon hearing the apology, he found he didn't much care after all. "Is it only me you're rousing, do you think?"

Alastair's head tilted slightly, his dark eyes quizzical as he watched the sea too. "Don't know. I'm not dragging phantom chains or clanking the pipes or howling. At a guess, if it *is* me, it's just you and Benson who are at the disadvantage."

"Well," said David, eyeing the edge of shore, "it sort of felt to me like you're howling. Not just shuffling and pacing."

Taking a breath, something David would never

consider strange even though it was, Alastair tutted softly. "Nah, that... that's not me."

"You feel it, too, then?" David had not considered it.

This most recent visit to The Shuck felt physically different from all the others. Everyone seemed louder, for a start. But David had first attributed the difference to his own bewitchment lifting, as well as his tiredness: so much had occurred in the last month that he convinced himself any differences he perceived must be only psychological in their nature, the result of fatigue and elation, things once hidden coming to the fore.

Choices made, too. Uncomfortable, he brushed away the sudden consideration of Ralph as though he'd walked through an errant cobweb in a corridor.

"Whatever existence I'm in, I think it leaves me more open to... fuck knows. Energy? Souls, maybe?" Alastair's teeth caught on a bit of dead skin on his lower lip.

David rubbed his face. "There's another ghost here?"

At that, Alastair chuckled. "Don't sound so dismayed. No."

He looked at David, and in that instant, David understood why a young Paul would grant this strange man access to his cellar. The angles of his face bathed in the same quiet light touching the room, Alastair said, "I can't be sure, but I think it's all the grief—all *his* grief—pent up. It's got to go somewhere. I reckon if you went to your own house or took a different room here, you could sleep." Tonguing the edge of his lip, just, he added, "It's diluted downstairs. But I like feeling it up here."

Beautiful as the thought was, it still struck David

as deeply sad. He would want to feel Lennie's grief, if that were all he could feel of them. "Did *I* trap it? Paul's grief?" If so, it was a wonder Paul let him anywhere within the vicinity.

"Mm, with your witchcraft? I'd bet not. Grief has a life of its own."

Alastair sounded like he spoke from experience of remorse or bereavement or something else, though David was too well-bred to push for more clarification. Reflecting, he looked again at the sea beyond the window. He had so rarely felt things happened with any propulsion of fate until now. Until he met Theo, his life had been an orderly sequence of events that seemed logical.

Father mentioned God, believed in God, and there were relatives who'd been religious too. But to David, God and whatever will he possessed never seemed mystical or spiritual, but rather more like a structured science. Likely due to the cold way Father spoke about everything. It had resulted only in atheism adopted out of some spite. Privately, David almost believed in *something.*

It was becoming more impossible by the day to believe in nothing.

If one went back far enough, there were the witch-hunter ancestors and likely more Puritans who were less aggressive in their pursuits. Perhaps, David reasoned, he was reclaiming belief from the poisoned well of bigotry. Although the Mills line had become quite practical and staid, it had originated from people who believed in things like witchery, and even Father had believed in demons in the Biblical sense.

In some manner, David felt more at peace being as he was now than he had been several weeks ago. Things were no longer logical, but he found he had more trust in what unfolded. No longer was he so anxious, so stretched thin.

He asked, feeling compelled to say it as he thought of witchery, demons, and Puritans, "Do you want to try something?"

"I'm a little limited in my capacity. But, why not?"

With a smile, for Alastair had not even asked what it was, David said, "That's the spirit."

"Is that a pun?"

David's smile slid into a small frown. He was not generally a punning sort of man. "Oh... no. I hadn't thought of it."

Hooking his thumbs in his pockets, Alastair smirked. "What are you thinking?"

"Well," David said. "I'll play medium." Benson had alluded to it, staunchly maintaining that speaking to the ghosts was all well and good, but anything more shouldn't be tolerated. He didn't *say*, though, that it was impossible. *Or that it can't be done on purpose.* Even when last David had thought about it, the possibility was there.

LENNIE GRADUALLY CAME AWAKE to the sound of David speaking with what they would classify as some manner of Edinburgh accent. First, they thought they were in a dream—an odd one, to be sure. Though it was not troubling, it could not fit any reality they were accustomed to. Many things came naturally to David, or so it seemed to them, but mimicry was not one.

He must have a guest and Lennie was hearing them, their sleepy mind blurring the two tones as they woke.

Blinking, they sat up in bed and listened to the

talking that drifted in from the room beyond. Paul's rustic parlor was small, but not as small as the other two rooms he occupied. As Paul and Lennie well knew, at least three people could easily fit within it and move about freely.

"This is a fair bit more than channeling or mediumship." It was David's voice, yet more than, the consonants and vowels belonging to someone else entirely. The tone itself remained his. Lennie waited and continued to listen, puzzling over what transpired. "I'm sorry. I certainly didn't mean to."

"No," said David, and this time it felt more familiar to Lennie. The same voice streaked with Cambridge propriety, even if it was rather strained at the moment. The one that held the power to make them blush as they both lounged together in early morning light. "I suggested it, and it isn't as though any of us have a guide to how this is done."

"True, but it does feel like a slight imposition. I'm not looking at your thoughts, by the way."

"Even if you did, I doubt you would find much you didn't already know."

"I was thinking automatic writing, perhaps, or some manner of..."

"No matter," returned the cadence of speech that sounded almost entirely like David. "I don't feel any the worse for wear. How does it feel for you?"

"Well, you're shorter than I was. Have to say it's odd being in this room and seeing it from a few less inches."

"Aside from that?" *That* flat resignation was all David.

With a grin, Lennie stepped out of the bed, their left foot resting on the cool wood floor before their right. Now that they had some idea of what had happened, given their well-rooted belief in the preternatural, it was not so bizarre a thought at all. If David and Benson were so similar, their witchery extending to the same arenas, it stood to reason David was up to something with Alastair.

Mum would have called it necromancy with no particular moral care either way. Although she believed in God, she'd never espoused anything to do with hellfire. The way she explained it, she couldn't. No self-respecting person would damn themself instead of allowing God to do it.

According to some, anyone who had visions of the future was no better than them who were led by the devil, and she was no such person.

If David was truly communing with a dead man, to Lennie it was no different from someone with excellent pitch singing, or anybody with an astute color sense painting.

"I smell your cologne." There, they imagined, was Alastair again, his spirit playing David the way a flautist might play their flute. "The smoke from last night's fire. Dust. The dregs in that empty teacup over on the sideboard..." David, who was more than David, David with a twinge of alien tones, halted his sentence and gasped. "Come on. I need to do something."

A rustle of cloth and hushed, bare footsteps on a timeworn wood floor, lighter than David's usually were, swept across the parlor toward the bedroom. Then the door opened and David was inside. They sat back down on the edge of the mattress.

One look into his eyes was enough for Lennie to know the truth of the situation.

"Hullo, Alastair," they said, trying to find it within

them to care that they were naked while someone other than their beloved looked out of his face, bringing a somewhat hawkish intensity to the fore that David did not ordinarily possess.

Truly, they could think of so many other things to mind. It wasn't as though they might need to think of their reputation. The Shuck was not the place for those kinds of sensibilities, at any rate. They gazed at David and took in the stance of his body, which they had come to know so well.

They noted how he stood, feet slightly apart in some semblance of parade rest, as though braced for slight impact.

"Morning," David said, though it was not David at all.

The parade rest did not last long after the single word's delivery, and David strode to the narrow wardrobe in the far corner, an old piece of furniture that had been scuffed and used for what appeared to be generations. It might have been here before any Apollyon had ever owned The Shuck, or it might have been one of the pieces Paul had accrued.

There were at least several chairs and a few assorted tables that had been rescued from the side of a road, or Thetford wood, or along the prom, and Tom had once mentioned a mirror that someone had left assuming it was cursed. Lennie did not think it was, for it possessed no special trail of colors and nothing else outside of ordinary perception marked it as such.

Intrigued, Lennie kept quiet while David, still clad in a nightshirt, swept open the wardrobe's doors and drew out an old, unlined coat the shade of bleached driftwood. An item of clothing for the height of summer by the look of it. Little else was inside, for it was apparent that Paul had actually taken most of his clothing with him to Edinburgh. Though he was not what Lennie would call poor, he seemed frugal in his approach to outfitting himself. The bedroom was rather bare of clothes and personal effects. There were a few things in the back of the wardrobe that they suspected had belonged to Alastair—they were faded black or maroon. David ignored them.

Whatever Lennie did expect to transpire, it was not for David to press the cloth to his nose and inhale deeply, revealing the action to Lennie mostly in profile as he remained half-turned to the open wardrobe.

But had they been dead for that long, then granted the ability to smell David's clothing, they would have done the same.

Suddenly, their heart felt bruised.

Feeling privileged to watch such a thing, they kept quiet as David—Alastair—clutched the lapels and all but stuffed them into his nostrils, inhaling as though he'd been half-suffocated and only just regained the ability to breathe.

When Alastair remained silent with his face partially buried in fabric, Lennie offered, "There are a few other things of Paul's here. I don't know how much an old summer coat would—"

"No, it does." Joy, unadulterated, laced through the reply. "It smells of him."

Too pleased for Alastair to dwell on how intimate it was to smell one's lover, Lennie said, "Good. We changed the linens on the bed after he left, otherwise I'd offer—"

Hearing this, Alastair seemed to recall the body he was using to experience such a small, but keen and grounding pleasure, was not his.

Abruptly, he murmured, "I should have asked."

"It's hardly the worst you could do, sniffing summer linens. I can't say I wouldn't do the same if I were in your shoes. Well, if I were in my present... bare feet serving as your proverbial shoes." *Those*, thought Lennie, were David's consonants and vowels. The ones that had at first intimidated them.

David came around the bed, bestowing a smile upon Lennie that was all him, reminiscent of the sun sparkling blindingly on a crisp morning. He drank from a partially filled glass on the bedside table. "I will say this has made my mouth *incredibly* dry." Finishing the water, he added with an air of quizzical inquiry, "Though, who is to say it's the cause?"

Quiet, Lennie eyed David, fascinated by the dualities playing on his face as two souls conversed with his mouth. There was nothing grotesque about it. But it had the slight effect of someone inexperienced trying to throw their voice.

"Possession, more like," said Lennie, after a moment. Considering it, they felt all of this was part of David's more innate preternatural state, the one he had been disregarding his whole life. Holding little by way of fear for the dead, they looked up at him. This did not feel alarming. If anything, David seemed galvanized. "Benson would run from the room howling."

They itched to know why the old man held such an aversion to the practices of necromancy when he was so knowledgeable in a bookish fashion.

Rather, Lennie would call it bookish if it were not to do with Benson.

Both fear and knowledge might coexist at the same time, and at first, Lennie had the sense Benson simply had been that way from the start, much the same way one might fear spiders for no logical motivation at all. There could be something primeval to it. Fearing the unrestful dead possibly made more sense than embracing them.

But as the days passed and Alastair became more perceptible and keen on innocent interactions with his fellow residents, Benson withdrew. It made Lennie reassess their initial conclusion; Benson's nervousness did not appear to be a normal, perhaps healthy, reaction to a ghost.

"We don't have to tell him."

"True," said Lennie. "Might be for the best." Sometime, though, he would likely find out.

Then Alastair seemed to notice their state of undress, for David blinked and averted his eyes, and muttered, "I shall leave you to it." It must have been Alastair more than David, who took to Lennie's nakedness with alacrity and had for the month they'd been cohabitating.

That month felt both longer and shorter to Lennie, who was starting to be of the opinion that so much of what occurred in their life before David was a sort of fever dream.

Chuckling, Lennie said, "Do what you like. For a ghost, you're polite. Not that I've met any before you."

"I just thought David might prefer it if I wasn't eyeing you."

"You were smelling Paul's coat, not eyeing me."

Unbothered, they stood and began to dress, perhaps wrongly assuming Alastair had encountered enough naked bodies in his presumably colorful life that it didn't matter. They did not imagine a free trader, a smuggler, had lived celibately before marrying. Lennie was sure his peers were not all of a decorous variety anyway.

Their own peers were hardly paragons of virtue,

and all they'd been was an ordinary pickpocket. Having lived so long on their own and possessing more or less the clothes on their back at any given moment, they were accustomed to wearing nothing or merely a shirt when they were alone.

Adapting to company or others' ideals did not come easily, although when it came to this particular one, the only person whom they had to consider was David. He'd compromised by offering Lennie the finest of kimonos for when Musgrave or another member of staff was underfoot. Quickly enough, they got dressed.

Then they asked, speaking to David's back as he examined a small mirror hung on the wall, edged in either pewter or tarnished silver, "What will you do now? I can't imagine going about all the things we need to do here with a ghost inside you will be..." they considered what word to choose. Something too dire would not fit, for they did not think David was in danger. But they did wonder at the effect upon his body. He was, after all, new to this, no matter how enthusiastically he appeared to be embracing it. "Easy."

Alastair's inflections surfaced through David's voice as David made a face into the mirror. "Christ, this is bizarre. I'm working you like a puppet." Then he turned. "Hm?"

"I don't know if you two should carry on for too long on your first go," said Lennie, smiling a bit at Alastair's incredulity. "What if it tires you out? I'm not Paul. You can't leave *me* alone to run The Shuck, not with Mrs. Lloyd still having her cold. I should have little notion of what to do." They also couldn't really advise Rose, the maid, for she had only worked there for a month and was still learning her way about.

"Hadn't thought of that. I am sure you could mind

it admirably," said David. It *was* him who answered. He sighed, more of a put-upon sigh than one of true fatigue. "Nothing I've read prepared me for this."

"I don't think books could prepare you for this," said Lennie, as gently as they could.

He was still learning that life, unlike what his Father had taught him, could not be fully navigated even with the help of the right kind of knowledge. Or self-discipline. There was simply no preparing for all of it, and in Lennie's experience, nothing worth discovering could be rehearsed. While the David of today had changed so much compared to the one they'd trailed along Gentleman's Walk, they suspected some of his habits wouldn't change.

Though he said his father forbade him from reading tawdry fiction and anything to do with folk-lore, there had been great emphasis placed upon suit-able topics for a Mills. Lennie noticed that the type of literature was the thing that had changed, not David's interest in consuming it.

"They're right," said Alastair-as-David. Briefly, Lennie wondered if Alastair knew how to refer to them because he could read David's own mind. They couldn't recall ever overtly discussing it in a situation where Alastair might overhear, even given the eaves-dropper that he was. Most everyone else in The Shuck had addressed them as a man until more recently.

Then again, he is clever.

He'd probably noticed Paul or the others not using he, and made the inference himself.

Because it interested them, they just asked. "How do you know to say that?"

"You do seem like the sort of person who is often right."

Offering him a half-smile, they replied, "I knew you were clever. But, no. They."

"I know that's what you meant. Just picked it up from Paul." David lifted a shoulder in a nonchalant shrug that was far too nonchalant for him alone. "Not for me to question it."

Lennie's smile grew. Then they nodded to David. "Can you see inside his head? I thought you might know from that, too."

"If I try. It's fucking strange. I'm not trying much, but there *is* some bleed-through even when I don't."

"See, I don't know how any of this would get written down in some kind of, what? A how-to-get-possessed instructional book? You'd be locked away for insanity." They'd thought far more than they'd like about being locked up for such things, because Ralph had regularly threatened them with it.

"Frankly, I'm enjoying this, but I don't want to hurt you." Alastair was addressing David, now. "My mother always told me all sorts of stories when I was a boy, about witches and ghosts and selkies..."

"Theo will be thrilled to hear it," remarked Lennie.

"One of them that I remember keenly, and I've had so much time to think about it since coming back," continued Alastair with the barest hint of a smirk, "is about a type of person she called a taibhsear."

Lennie, having no familiarity with Gaelic past knowing what it was when they heard it, waited for him to elaborate. Their lack of knowledge must have shown in their expression, for he chuckled and continued quickly enough.

"I suppose they're a seer. Only they speak with the dead. It's not a direct translation—I didn't speak Gaelic like she and my grandparents did. My father didn't encourage it. But in the tales she told, these ones seemed to attract ghosts. And things weren't always easy for them."

Intrigued upon hearing this allusion to folklore, Lennie said, "Then if you'd kindly get out of him?"

It was one thing to experiment. Experimentation had always been of interest to them and it might even be credited with allowing them to come into their own. Without trying new things they thought would work, they might never have confirmed certain suspicions about who they were and loved. Somehow, the suggestion of trial and error felt more dangerous when it involved David's wellbeing. They loved him too much.

Though, in the back of their mind, they admitted they didn't believe he was in much danger from his new forays into the occult. Mum had to be thanked for their pragmatism in that respect. She'd never treated it as anything to be overly frightened of, and so Lennie was rarely scared of magic for its own sake.

Still, there was a possibility that David might overextend himself. They crossed their arms and attempted not to scowl, especially when they realized David—Alastair—still clutched Paul's linen coat. His attachment to Paul, as well as his very human attraction to certain sensations, like scent, made it difficult to deny him the chance to sniff.

The moment Alastair left David seemed subtle enough. There were small flickers in the air not unlike the spark that had travelled between David and Robbie, the same one that had seen Robbie out cold. Then David's knees buckled.

"Shit, that is mad. A mad feeling," said David faintly, but what amused Lennie was how delighted he actually sounded.

Now that David Mills had a taste of the preternatural, and indeed was an odd channel for it, it seemed he rather enjoyed the thrill.

They came forward with resignation and eased him to the bed. "At least Alastair listened to me, I suppose. Come on, lay down before you fall and hit your head on something hard."

9

I f Tom thought everything would be well upon returning home, he was mistaken. Knowing it was all askew might have seen him lingering longer and consoling Paul as best he could in Scotland. But it had seemed best to leave Portobello before Paul could hit more of its residents, and they had done so the morning after that tense little fracas.

In truth, it was difficult to see what resolution there could be to the situation with Mr. Gow, if any. Nobody on either end of the conflict could be satisfied, and everyone's actions after Alastair's death had been motivated by some manner of desperation or an acute emotion. Clearly, Mr. Gow was still deeply hurt by his adoptive father's choices. After all, he had been so during the only time he'd visited Cromer and Tom didn't think it would abate.

Paul, meanwhile, had been so compromised by grief that he'd made stark choices.

He had elected to shutter his own magic; he had chosen to cling to a man who was no longer there. He'd let that absence dictate his every move.

Neither response was rational, but they were made all the worse by Paul's inability to grieve in a concrete manner at a place where such grief was permitted in the open.

Alastair had not been lost at sea, after all. He'd been taken away. Either circumstance would be torturous, Tom was sure, but one was pointedly cruel. The other, chance.

No matter how justified Tom believed Paul had been in hitting Mr. Gow, he needed rest and to return to his routines more than he needed to bruise Alastair's son's face. Little else beyond normalcy would help, save perhaps the support of those who'd gathered around him.

But until Paul wished to take it, their concern wouldn't matter, and he had been decidedly avoiding most conversation since their return three days prior. It was possible he had taken their discussion before Mr. Gow's intrusion to heart; Tom hoped he was engaging in gentle self-reflection and letting down his defenses against premonitions.

While Tom was no seer, and didn't consider himself much of a witch no matter what Benson or anybody else said, he had an unshakable sense of two things. One, that *something* was about to happen, and secondly, that it had to do with Alastair being within The Shuck. By extension, Alastair and Paul's fates felt entwined to him.

Tom locked the main door behind himself, knowing it was operable from the other side should anybody wish to venture out at night. The lock had been specially commissioned by his grandfather.

He breathed a sigh of relief, and said to Theo, "I could use a walk."

He couldn't even countenance what they might have to eat before retiring to bed, but the thought of strolling along the water appealed greatly. Food could wait.

Remarkably little was going easily for the permanent residents of the place. It had not collapsed, it had not flooded or burnt, which were blessings to be counted. But Benson's lingering cold had ebbed to leave him breathing like a squelching bog, and Mrs. Lloyd could still not taste a thing, which rendered her grumpy and impacted their supply of cakes. Meanwhile, David had taken to bed upstairs. Lennie was being remarkably closed-lipped about it given their usually blunt temperament.

Caught the cold, too, Tom supposed.

To top it all off, Paul had reverted to his intense seclusion.

This had never been a place of etiquette or propriety. But it all felt a bit mad, rather like some satirist had penned absurd scripts for them and they were playing parts.

"Then, by all means." Theo, as ever almost capable of reading his mind, nodded gently in the sea's direction. Carefully, Tom took his uninjured hand and they walked in the quiet darkness to the promenade, then down to the beach.

Things were never deathly silent, though, especially in summer. Whether gulls cried to each other, or people, unseen from their vantage point, carried on loud conversations yards and yards in the distance, there was a constant sense of being accompanied.

"What was the point of going to Edinburgh?" Tom asked, when they were just by the water's edge.

Theo, apparently heedless of whoever might happen to pass by, removed his shoes and socks. He walked right toward the edge of the lapping waves. "Things don't have to have a point." He expertly rolled his socks so they were tucked into his shoes, then kept an easy grip on the shoes. "I guess it was good for him to understand Mr. Gow is always going to be bitter. But even that doesn't have to serve a purpose."

"No. But I thought going would help him, and now he's just worse."

"You don't know that. Maybe he's up in his flat having visions again."

"Maybe he's up in his flat letting it become as bad as it was, again."

"It's life," Theo said kindly. "Movement may not look like movement. But don't immediately think the worst thing."

As soothing as it could be to love a preternatural creature whose identity he would never quite understand, it was also like speaking to an exceedingly philosophical old man at times. At Theo's core, Tom supposed he was such a man. *Not that I shall ever see him look old.*

"And I've never heard of David taking to his bed over a cold, before," said Tom, relaying none of his thoughts about Theo never looking old while they both still lived. It was an idea he'd grappled with since last winter. But seeing as Theo could do little about it, Tom endeavored to be happy he had met such a lover. He didn't wish to fret over what he could not have due to the realities of the situation. "And for it to be so bad that he can't go to either of his own houses."

"You didn't live with him."

"What?"

His tone arch, Theo said, "He's an *infant* when he has a cold. I don't envy Lennie. David does go to bed when he's not feeling quite the thing. He complains. Then you bring him tea, and he complains a little less."

"Well... you would know." Tom glanced at Theo's free hand. It bore nothing horrendous, but the candle's flame had eventually roused a small blister and redness on the surrounding skin. While he had a longer lifespan than most and did not seem to age at the same rate, he wasn't capable of miraculous healing. He did usually recover more quickly than Tom from cuts or bruises, so maybe the burn *was* shaping up at a rate quicker than anything termed natural. But it was subtle. "How is it?"

"My palm?"

"Yes, love."

"Eh, it's on the mend. Just lucky I'm not left-handed, I suppose."

Curiously, for he did not ask too many questions of Theo when it concerned his own inner life, Tom said, "If you were to change. Would the injury follow you?" Aware of how fearful Theo was of being controlled or coerced, Tom left it at one question. He didn't wish to force Theo into divulging more than he felt comfortable saying, and most days, he was content with what he was given.

Theo appeared to consider it. Then he said, "Well, that would be something to find out, would it not?" He beamed impishly at Tom, whose heart sped up at the sight. "Want to find out with me?"

"What, right here?" Tom, not ankle-deep in the water as Theo was, looked over his shoulder toward the promenade and all the buildings with their windows. It seemed an undue risk, particularly during a busy season.

Theo ambled back to him, smug as a cat with its cream, and pressed his shoes into his hands. "Hold these."

"Are you serious?"

"No, I'm curious. I've never changed when I've been injured."

Tom assumed if he was being handed shoes and socks, all of Theo's garments were to follow. "And your clothes?" Aghast, Tom gazed at him and couldn't even appreciate the flush of his cheeks or the glint in his eyes. "You'd have to stay a seal to avoid arrest if you don't have those."

Laughing, Theo said his name like a talisman. "Silence, they stay on."

This did not match anything he had read at all. But there were many things that did not match what he'd read. Theo was not a woman, for example. For he had not come across anything written about male selkies, either. They obviously existed: Theo's abilities even came from his father, not his mother. But the thought of his clothes somehow melting away when he became a seal, then returning to his person when he went back to being a man pushed Tom's reasoning.

"Do they?"

"Yes. And I *do* have my skin on my person, if you wondered."

"Why? I mean to say, why do your clothes stay on?"

"I don't know," said Theo, serenity exuding from his demeanor.

Quizzical, Tom abandoned his reticence to ask questions. "Did your father know why?"

"No."

"Are you soaked through to the skin when you change back?"

"Well, I wouldn't say I'm drenched, but... wet. Yes."

"Do you think anyone knows the answer to this shit?"

Theo kissed his cheek. "Maybe someone, somewhere. Or perhaps we just need to make our peace without knowing the *why*." His eyes searched Tom's face, and Tom could only imagine how confused he looked to Theo. "Darling, we can walk a little more down that way, which is not as near to the promenade. I *doubt* anybody will happen to look out their window at the exact moment I walk into the water."

"I'm not worried about them seeing a man go into the water, even clothed. I'm worried about somebody putting it together that—"

"They'd really have to be looking and waiting. Come along." Theo beckoned him. On they walked, until a small curve would hide them from most views. Under private circumstances, Tom might have been more eager. He tried to summon the image of a seal within their cottage. It seemed all of his protective instincts voiced their opinions when Theo might expose himself as a preternatural being.

"Don't look so tense," said Theo, his expression kind. "I know what you're thinking, and a seal in the sitting room wouldn't be at all desirable. I would probably break something, and I'd be much too hot in a house."

Even Tom had to chuckle at the thought of such an animal indoors. "Yes, well, David did almost harm you by separating you from your skin. I would rather nobody else ever had the chance."

"I know," said Theo, and the two words' composure carried all the weight of his calm assurance. He grinned and released a breath. "Ready?"

Scowling, Tom looked out at the water, watching whitecaps form and shift. "No."

"Good lad."

With that, Theo ventured into the sea. His pace was not leisurely.

Tom had often suspected the water did call to him. He sometimes wondered if it felt more like a home than anything he and Theo had created, but the thought did not generally stay with him for long unless he was having a bad, inky day. Faulting Theo for that would be like faulting a cat for eating meat.

At last, Theo properly swam, then dove, and the dexterity he exhibited just as a man made it clear how he could have rescued Tom from the water all those months ago. Until they were better acquainted—and even then—Tom had questioned how he could manage a feat that some whose job it was to rescue others from drowning could not.

When a seal's head bobbled up in the next moment, Tom was not surprised. He was, however, a bit stunned when his eyes met the seal's limpid black ones. There was nothing remarkable about the creature. It appeared just like the many seals Tom had seen. The only exception might be that its gaze was minutely too intelligent.

For anyone who did not know what they gazed upon, the nuance could be easily explained away.

He waited, and smiled, as the seal came to shore and arranged itself rather like a person would lounge. The moon was not entirely full, but allowed enough light for Tom to see the brindled flecks in his fur, as well as both of his front flippers with some clarity.

He assumed, anyway, that front flippers were analogous to hands. When both of the front flippers wiggled, first one, then the other, he smiled. "Right, I know."

Theo huffed at him through a seal's nose, as he knelt and carefully examined both of them. Neither was injured, which *did* surprise Tom a little. "This is... extraordinary."

But the lack of injury also brought a deep twinge of guilt. If Theo could heal so much better in this state, Tom hoped it was not unhealthier for him to remain a man the majority of the time. Needing the comfort, he reached out and pressed the tip of his finger to the edge of Theo's flipper.

"You should change back," he said, his words barely audible over the surf.

Nonetheless, Theo heard him, and where Tom might have thought he'd trundle back to the water, he instead changed right there. It happened in the space of a blink or a breath, and there was no alteration to Theo's usual signature of colors, no flares or eddies of sparks in the air. In a way, Tom was more awed by the sheer ordinariness of it than he would have been by a preternatural show of flickers and lights.

Theo beamed up at him, the palm of his hand extended to just touch Tom's pointer finger. "Happy you wondered and thought to ask, for I'm good as new."

"I just thought, because you seem to be a quicker healer than me anyway, perhaps... it might not necessarily accompany you in a seal form." Tom got to his feet and offered Theo a hand up without looking directly at him.

"What is it?"

"Nothing."

"Tom," said Theo, "I know that look." Tom could not imagine the *look* or what it appeared to connote. He assumed it merited concern for Theo to sound so conciliatory. He resolutely shrugged.

"I think we should get inside. You're wet, and the sun is down. True, it isn't December or January, but all the same." As he spoke, he held Theo's hand and caressed his palm, struggling with how to put into words the inadequacy he felt compared to magic and the sea.

He wasn't sure if fragility was a reasonable price to pay for his love, and tried to tell himself that it was only Theo's choice to make.

After all, even if Theo did not know if an injury would be directly healed by the preternatural powers he possessed, he still must have realized there were exchanges to be made to have a normal life. At the moment, it didn't occur to Tom to simply *ask* if he'd already decided being a man was preferable.

Tom neglected to remind himself that Theo had spent great spans of time this way.

It felt like Tom Apollyon was a rather poor prize indeed for a man who'd witnessed decades of change and could read the human heart like a favorite book. Theo Harper was, in essence, extraordinary.

They might have laughed had Robbie not physically threatened Paul in his own home. As Lennie came into the foyer, Paul faced Robbie—and Robbie faced Paul. He looked quite grateful that a stretch of desk separated them. Paul was not a large man, standing below six feet and remaining quite trim, while Robbie himself could only be described as hulking. Still, Robbie had the air of a cornered rabbit. It was just as well, thought Lennie.

I'm more wary of Paul than Robbie. Even if Paul had not managed to knock him out, he would be much more intimidating in their opinion.

"He's asleep," Paul said.

"Why the hell are you here?" Lennie asked, by way of greeting. They placed a stack of clean linens on the large desk, having been on their way up to Rose, who was turning over the rooms.

"Why are you still here if *he's* here?" Robbie, always mulish, nodded with his chin toward Paul. "And I assumed you'd be in Norwich if your man was here."

"Unlike you, I'm a welcome addition to The Shuck's milieu." They'd learned what the word meant several days ago and liked the sound of it. Their milieu had expanded and improved. "Why are *you* here if your dear papa is ailing?"

Rather evasively, Robbie said, "I need to talk to him. David. Mr. Mills."

"So badly that you needed to do so in person?" Paul said.

"Well," said Lennie. "You've wasted the trip. He's ailing, himself."

Whatever David recovered from was not catching, and he was quite cheerful even if he was dead tired. It was probably the result of letting Alastair occupy his body. Still, Lennie had not decided if they would ask Benson or anyone else about a taibhsear. Theo might be the next most logical person given his origin, and he was infinitely more approachable.

But when they considered whether they should peruse the conversation, they knew they did not really need to ask—if David could house a spirit that was not his own, if he could see and hear spirits, he fit the vague description. In the end, it did not change much, for he already was what he was.

Alastair had merely supplied a new word for a concept Lennie already knew. Like milieu.

For the moment, rather than blurt out anything about magic, they merely huffed as Robbie gave them a look of perplexity.

"What's wrong with him?"

"He's just unwell, is all," said Lennie. They wanted to ask if this was a planned call. It seemed otherwise.

That David was unwell, at least, was true. He was exceedingly sleepy and sounded like he had a slight cold. They had no doubt he would recover. But they weren't keen on Alastair reenacting the same circumstances for at least several days. They had been clear with the ghost on that point, talking to seemingly empty rooms that they knew were not empty.

"Come on. You can talk to me if you wish, but you'll have to follow me upstairs." They added, "The customary way, not the back way."

Even Robbie had the grace to appear daunted and somewhat regretful in response to the addition. It pleased Lennie. His broad shoulders slumped a little and he awarded Paul with a nearly apologetic glance.

Paul gave a dry cough, which Lennie had realized was his manner of covertly chuckling, then waved them both off as though dismissing a pair of court jesters.

Reaching carefully for the linens, Lennie picked them up again. Without waiting for Robbie, they started for the stairs. "I quite liked working here while the Apollyons and Mr. Harper went to Edinburgh. Find things still run smoother if I pitch in." What they did not say was David had elected to sleep here rather than his own house because he was too tired to relocate.

But Robbie did. "He *must* be ill, then, if he ain't using his house with its views of the sea."

"Don't get any ideas."

"He's already given me enough to keep us both for a month or two. I've no need to steal from him."

Pausing on the first landing, Lennie tilted their head and didn't want to reveal David hadn't told them he'd done so, specifically. They supposed the account for business was different from David's personal one, so they would not have necessarily seen the money move. It mightn't be pernicious at all.

They hadn't liked the idea of David stepping in

instead of them when it came to the original amount to be paid, and had directly said so. Grudgingly, they supposed he hadn't. Not if they considered the technicalities: they'd given Robbie the money. After that, anything David supplied himself didn't go against their wishes.

"Right, I'd forgotten." And Robbie's *us* had to have meant Ralph and Robbie.

If Robbie thought Lennie was irked, he didn't say. He did seem to sense their overall unease, however. In his way, he attempted to be comforting. "Well, I'm sure he'll pull through. He's young. Strong for a toff."

Left unaddressed was how Robbie knew David's strength: a spark to the chest that had rendered him unconscious. Lennie had possessed few theories as to why it'd happened, until these last few days. Whatever David had done then, it must be intimately allied to his abilities to communicate with Alastair, and the magic he was navigating.

Lennie wasn't as steeped in theories of the preternatural as David; their experience was more lived or familial. But they could follow links between life itself and the souls who might remain after it had expired, and it appeared David had an affinity for those particular energies. Mum might have been more astute and they would've given so much to ask her about it.

Paul might be able to provide a similar perspective, too. But Lennie did not want to pressure him overmuch, as his return from Edinburgh seemed to leave him quite wan. Though he didn't fully disappear, as had apparently been his habit before they knew him, he was keeping more to himself. Benson was venturing upstairs to speak with him. It wasn't always easy to account for Benson's habits, but the two men were friends, and the latter was heartwarmingly protective in his way.

"I haven't a doubt. And he's strong for anyone, not only a toff."

"If you say so," said Robbie.

Lennie bit their lower lip to keep from grinning. While David wasn't an extremely active sort, he did exhibit physical prowess in bed. Robbie needn't know that, though. They knocked on the doorframe before entering the room Rose was tidying, and left the linens on a chair.

When they'd ducked back into the corridor, they said, "What'd you need to talk to David about? If I can be so nosy."

It might be employment of some kind. David did not like Robbie. Lennie didn't think he ever would, but Lennie quickly discovered *they* were David's weakness and he seemed ready to help their family for no reason other than the relation itself. Lennie knew it was largely to keep Ralph or Robbie from being a nuisance. Ralph had harassed, manipulated, or extorted Lennie for years. Robbie himself contributed far less to any of those categories, but he had never impeded his father, either. From David's perspective, it was tantamount to a cardinal sin.

Still, since he had a warm heart even if it was obscured by layers of fine cloth and hereditary propriety, David might well try to help Robbie seek better and more consistent employment than his presently dubious variety.

If he did, he'd say it was to keep Robbie out of the way, of course. But Lennie would know that even if that was part of the truth, it was also because David felt for an underdog. While he might rather wear the same wardrobe for the next two decades than admit it,

Lennie felt David saw at least a little of himself reflected in Robbie.

"Oh, just a job."

It was the answer they expected. Yet something about it nagged at them. They'd long since stopped attuning themself to Robbie because it felt like spying. But for the first time in an age, they itched to follow that nagging sensation.

"He has a lot of connections," Lennie said.

Robbie leaned his back against one of the old beams that held up the walls and ceiling. He seemed to be evaluating them to glean a level of understanding, only Lennie wasn't privy to what he wanted to understand. Confusion flitted onto his face, plain enough to see. "And I'm very grateful to him."

"What kind of work has he helped you find, then?"

Conflict crept into Robbie's voice. "He hasn't."

Now *that* was interesting. "You just said 'a job,' though."

On a sigh, Robbie said, "Lennie, you have to let it go." He sounded, for the first time they had ever noted when he spoke to them, rueful.

"What do you mean?" They felt the frown contort their face.

Never had Robbie told them to let anything go. Generally, most people of their acquaintance knew not to suggest it. The suggestion might, in fact, induce the opposite effect.

He ran a hand through his blond hair, resettling his old tweed cap as he did. "It's a private matter."

"How the hell can it be a private matter? You and he aren't close. You're not even friends. He only speaks to you because of me."

"Lennie..."

"Are you having a laugh?"

"No."

"You're not *pressuring* him, are you?"

Although Robbie had said there was no need to break into David's home, there were a wealth of other things he could turn his mind to. A lifetime of strife hadn't treated him well. Lennie believed he could learn to behave differently, but old habits were difficult to break. Particularly when one's father had been their architect.

The Mills family was not famous or so socially connected as to draw national interest. No one was notable. But they *were* wealthy; Robbie knew it. It would be misguided and rash for him to try something like blackmail—but David wasn't customary in his affections. Theo told Lennie in confidence that before he and David were involved, David *tried* stepping out with a woman.

Like watching a man with sand in his tea instead of sugar, Theo had said.

All the same, social expectations were a strong inducement. Yet they hadn't been strong enough for this association to turn into an engagement; David soon found himself in the arms of his secretary, a soft-spoken man from Leith.

Such affection was generally hidden from the public in most respects. It was, in David's case, hidden in every respect unless one knew how to see it. Or had a reason to look for it.

For someone like Robbie who'd been raised to follow opportunism, weaknesses like this were easy to sniff out. Studying him, Lennie tried to decide if their stepbrother would double back on his current path of apparent respectability. Ralph did not seem long for this world, and his father was indeed one factor in Robbie's poor behavior.

Once Ralph was gone, he might well find himself able to be a different person. Beyond that, Robbie seemed genuinely cowed by David and to some extent, Paul. Still, Lennie didn't know if he'd actually remain subdued. They didn't think Ralph had rotted all of Robbie's soul, but it wasn't easy to trust their step-brother given his father's noxious influence.

"Well?" they prompted, for Robbie had fallen quiet.

At that, he appeared to debate with himself. Lennie couldn't imagine the debate was particularly erudite or nuanced given who was having it. But it seemed urgent. Despite being more or less a criminal, Robbie had never learned to guard his facial expressions as well as he ought. Perhaps he didn't need to, for what he lacked in finesse, he made up for in stature.

At last, and after some palpable internal struggle, he murmured, "Just remember, it's for you."

That was no answer. "The fuck are you on about? I asked if you were pressuring him—that's not something I'd want, and I don't need anything from you."

His cheeks went pink, probably with leeching anger. Lennie knew his temper had always been rather short and didn't expect that would prove any different now.

"I'm not blackmailing your precious boy."

"Then what *are* you doing?"

"Leave it," said Robbie. "Please. All I can say is, it's for you. He's doing it for you." Then he brushed past Lennie and walked down the stairs with all the prac-ticed silence of a competent cat burglar, his size not mattering a bit. He called up to them, just as his head was disappearing around the landing, "Let him know I've called. It wasn't a scheduled visit, anyway."

Gazing after him, Lennie puzzled over what David could possibly be doing *for them* that he hadn't already done. Something about the suggestion made the hairs on the back of their neck stand up. They doubted the sensation had anything to do with being inside a haunted pub.

11

D espite being raised to view the natural world as somewhat primal and often frightening, deep down, David supposed he loved the sea. He would often invent excuses to run down to the beach when he, Mother, and Father stayed in the Cromer house. He'd spend hours near the waves as a child.

As he grew older and better at swimming, he'd float on his back in the water and close his eyes under the sun if he was so lucky that it was unencumbered by clouds. This felt like one of those immortal summer evenings—though the family had usually wintered by the sea, in an odd reversal of what others did, there were a few holidays of the summer variety.

Summer's energy was different; the Mills' stringent routines seemed softened by the combined vivacity of so many visitors to the seaside. That might have been why they did not spend every summer at the seaside.

He took a long, contented breath. Then, he looked to his left and saw someone who was decidedly not of his past at all. Alastair walked to meet him, leaving a trail of heavy prints in the sand with his boots.

"Did you choose this?" he called.

David didn't know what he meant. "What?"

"It's lovely."

"What's lovely?"

"Lovely setting for a dream."

A dream? David glanced to his left. Behind him, the shore gradually rose into a modest overlook. He looked right and saw nothing but the beach. If he looked forward, the ocean called.

Their surroundings appeared real as anything.

Perhaps the sounds were somewhat blunted and the sky was lurid as a painting. But David had spent many hours on this particular stretch and always fancied it might be close to perfection on earth. So even if it did look as pristine as a master's work of art, he wouldn't necessarily think he was in an otherworldly or mental rendition of it. "I'm still asleep, then."

Sitting on the rocks and sand, looking up at him, Alastair said, "Indeed, you are."

Feeling resignation of a sort he found was familiar in his dealings with the preternatural, David sat heavily. "How much longer will I be this tired?" A mild sense of remorse took the fore, for he knew Lennie must be worried.

"Not sure. But I've been told to let you rest a bit."

"Who told you that?"

"Lennie." Alastair smiled. "More than once. They said they'd stop leaving out Paul's letters, and I'm really not through enough of the pile. Low blow."

"I hope they're not too concerned. You don't seem to be."

"I've learned enough from Benson, for a start, to understand magic has its costs. If you ignore it—there's a cost. It's better not to ignore it."

David snorted. He well knew that cost. "I'm not, now."

"Yet, if you overindulge, so to speak—it also costs." Alastair rolled his eyes. "He says. Everything costs, if you talk to him. But that might be what you've done, for my money."

"It's the morning after drinking too much." David smiled to himself. It seemed he had a habit of overindulging, these days; he thought of wandering to Tom and Theo's under the influence of some aged whisky he'd spirited from Paul's stores years ago. It had been his first instance of such drunkenness in a long time. He could sympathize with Paul's bibulous, erratic flight to another place.

Alastair sighed as he looked out at the waves. "I suppose. Something like that. But it does seem you've been able to do all this strange shit for ages." David had not told him much, but it did not matter if a ghost could see inside his mind.

"Why are you in my dream?"

"Ah, that," said Alastair. "I'm practicing."

"How does it work?"

The logistics, the details, as always, fascinated David.

There were gaggles of learned men who devoted their time and efforts to understanding all manner of things like ghosts and hauntings. Largely with the goal of disproving them.

Suppositions had been made about the scientific aspects of the preternatural. David did and could not consider himself a skeptic, but these possibly scientific explanations still intrigued him. He supposed he just had a different motivation for wanting to learn about them.

"I don't know. I only know it works." Alastair grinned. "That's how I lived most of my life, anyway. Don't know, but it should work, let's do it."

The smile was infectious; David chuckled. "Fine. So, you're practicing because you want to talk to Paul, of course. Practice on everyone. He seems like he'll be last to fall." Upon a little reflection, though, he didn't know if that was the truth of the matter any longer.

He'd been in bed when Tom, Theo, and Paul returned from Scotland. All of them spoke so blasted quietly that he'd overheard very little of their conversations, if any. Lennie could be counted upon to display their emotions more openly. But unfortunately, Tom and Theo had wished to go home; Paul wished to go upstairs.

Lennie had told David as much when they'd come to check on him. It seemed everyone was too fatigued to debrief properly.

Even Tom, whose moods could be more capricious, took more after his uncle and rarely raised his voice. Theo, meanwhile, was urbane and given to soft speaking. So David did not know what kind of state Paul had come home in, or indeed, if the others had unearthed whether he was actually tamping down his own abilities.

However, Alastair went on to suggest something *had* happened.

He nearly quivered with an excitement that was tangible to David. "He's not as shuttered, not as distant, from me. I can tell."

"Really?" Then Theo must have spoken to Paul, as David had said he should.

"It's like being a moth drawn to a flame, I imagine." Alastair sighed. "He just feels warmer. Brighter, if you can imagine it. I don't think he'll ever see me in the waking world. Never could do that, him." After a pause, he said, "But dreams? That'll be my best way, I feel."

"We'll all help as we can."

"You already have. I think the letters have been helping because they strengthen the ties between us, somehow, and I'm sure he realized something or other while he was in Portobello." Serenity filled his voice, then dissipated. "I overheard them all carrying on about my son. Can't imagine any meeting went well if the one here, just after I'd died, is any indication." David knew better than to enquire more deeply about the matter of Alastair's adoptive son. "Oh, and you'll want to know why I chose you to practice on."

"Well..." It seemed obvious. He could not say the Gaelic word even though Alastair had used his mouth to utter it, but as a witch-hunter whose talents leaned toward the dead, David imagined he would be the ripest candidate for this exercise. After all, Alastair had also already used him. The connection had to exist.

He was about to say something along these lines.

Alastair preceded him. "Robbie, that bastard, was here to talk to you today."

Ire flared immediately. "Why? I wasn't expecting to manage the pub this past week, and I've told him we can't possibly plan anything at The Shuck, not with Lennie... I bet he's succumbing to nerves." He'd been waiting for Robbie to go back on their words about killing his father, mostly because he wouldn't trust Robbie's fortitude in any situation. "Wonder if he came to try to call it off."

Why else would he come in person?

It was either that, David was convinced, or possibly news that Ralph had either worsened or improved. Father's last few years had been littered with contradicting signs of improvement and decline. Overall, it had seemed that the incremental improvements to his health were actually harbingers of the end.

As though to stay him, Alastair held up a palm. "I understand why you don't want to tell Lennie. Killing, even killing an absolute brute... it changes you, and it changes how others see you."

"Thank you. But what happened? Something must have, or you wouldn't be here." For a shining instant, David truly hoped Ralph had just passed naturally.

"Robbie didn't tell Lennie anything, exactly. They *were* pressing him. Not that he's so eloquent. But he said, 'He's doing it for you.' I eavesdropped outside one of the rooms."

"So? That isn't terrible." He did feel a large measure of shame for keeping the secret from Lennie. But part of his plan was precisely to maintain that it had happened by natural causes. He winced as he thought of how he could go about such a thing. Poisons could be untraceable, and anyway, the sudden death of a very ill man would not be regarded with suspicion.

But even after Ralph was dead—if he'd died by David's hand, no matter what method—David would have to consider taking it to his own grave.

He was brought away from his gnarled thinking by Alastair's voice. "It made me think of something that might be amenable to you."

Looking over at him, David shrugged as best he could from his seated position. He was unsure what Alastair could offer him. "Well?"

"Lennie was right, I should think. What we did, it's possession."

Rather wondering where Alastair was headed, David said, "Yes, and?" He did not reveal he'd contemplated the idea of possession himself, and also didn't announce that he'd prefer to remain without tattoos.

"Robbie upsets me because of what he did to Paul. Still, I don't think he deserves to die. I just liked it when you scared him." Alastair's smirk was wicked, then his expression sobered. "But the more I've gleaned about his father, the more I think such a person shouldn't be entitled to life."

Perhaps being a ghost made one's morality more morbid. Then again, David had already felt his own grow more skewed. At length, he said, "He's a dastardly man." He'd forgotten that Alastair had been around for more than one discussion about Ralph.

"I've had a hand in ending better men than him."

"You don't have hands, now."

"No, but I could use yours."

A succession of waves lapped and ebbed as David took Alastair's meaning. He could not decide if the two of them paired together in one body would absolve him from murder. Regardless of how bloodless any mode of purposeful killing was, the result would be the same, and he would be the one to have carried it to a conclusion. "Would that really provide any distance between me and the act itself?"

"If you aren't directing yourself, I'm not sure if you're responsible."

David wasn't as convinced. "I appreciate the offer."

"I think you should consider it."

"Why?"

Alastair's air became more wolfish than David had seen it. "This seems to me more like a matter of justice than anything. But I've never been a decent man, so perhaps I shouldn't say."

Justice spoke to David, for that was how he viewed it, too. So little of his life until adulthood had been within his control. He'd felt trapped, forced to perform. He and Lennie were not fully alike in their experiences. He was not under that illusion. In means, in education, and in upbringings, they were dissimilar. He'd benefitted from much more than Lennie ever had. He was also in the privileged and straightforward realm of always appearing to others as he was.

He'd never needed to examine being a man. Or decide something did not match, then proceed with changing his presentation and ways.

But in his and Lennie's respective confinements to overbearing fathers' beliefs, they were comparable. David could not right his own father's wrongs. But he could go forward and end the only father Lennie had known, who had treated them abysmally and callously. He didn't think there was anything heroic about it; he didn't aim to be a hero. He wanted the source of Lennie's pain to be eliminated.

"I keep thinking it could be played off as natural."

"The best murders are."

David had to pause and ask, "Were you given to... habitually murdering?"

Tilting his head, Alastair replied, "As a young thing, I was part of certain environments where killing might take place. I didn't make it a habit. I *saw* more of it."

That's a delicate way of phrasing things.

"The older I got, the more removed I became from those circles. When I married, it didn't seem right to subject a wife to all the risk and worry, for one thing."

"But you're talking of murder as though we're planning a menu."

"For years, talking of murder *was* about that normal to me," said Alastair. "I came up in a world where it was eat or be eaten. I couldn't walk the walk as well as I talked the talk. But the latter protected me from having to walk *too* much."

"My world felt that way, too. Eat, or be eaten. Although I wager your stakes were much more dire."

"David, just let me help you help Lennie."

The seriousness in Alastair's voice roused questions in David's mind. He spoke as a man who didn't just want justice or rightness, but also as one who was a romantic. If he mentioned Lennie's name, he was thinking about them alongside David. Then, perhaps it did not need to be said that Alastair was given to flights of romance or passion.

Just look at where he is and what he's doing.

Before he'd renewed his acquaintance with the Apollyons, David was often tacitly jealous of Paul and his rumored paramour. Even when he was young, there had been unsavory words about the nebulous situation. David didn't know about all of it. Most of what he'd known was proven to be incorrect.

But anyone in his father's circles who might've referenced The Shuck, or Mr. Apollyon, made oblique mentions to whom he pined for. All spoken in hushed tones that connoted to David how inappropriate the pining was. There'd never been any illusions in his mind, at least, that a woman had broken Paul's heart. As an adult, he questioned if his father had allowed the implicit knowledge in order for it to serve as an example of what might happen should David choose to love the wrong person.

Love, by Father's measure, was never part of anything important. He'd said as much about marriage when David had first tentatively voiced his discomfort with the notion of a loveless union.

"Fine. You can kill Ralph. If he doesn't die on his own, first."

Pensive even in a dream state, David was uncertain what the agreement would entail. He did know that as soon as he woke, and as soon as he was able, he'd endeavor to take Alastair to Norwich as quickly as he could.

Who knew why Robbie had tried to pay him a visit today? Almost more pertinent than that, this was not a decision he wanted anyone else involved in—maintaining secrecy wasn't a new desire. Quickness would be of import.

In addition, he hardly wanted to lose his nerve.

He'd only started to prove he had it, and a man whose experience of the world was much harsher than his own had just asserted Ralph was not a good man at all. There could be no more time to lose.

"Lovely," said Alastair.

On a sigh, David asked, "Will you be able to leave The Shuck?"

Though this seemed like an elegant solution in many respects, it could melt like sugar in hot tea as soon as they made the attempt. Alastair had not been able to follow Paul. But perhaps if he was within another person's body, the logistics and rules, such as they were or whatever they might be, changed. More freedom of movement might be a reason why ghosts sought to possess the living.

Once again, David found himself irritated that Benson could be circumspect to the point of supplying nothing useful at all.

"Something tells me I can if you're carrying me like I'm in a boat."

"Something?"

"Yes," said Alastair. "I always heard grisly things about ghosts—demons, more like—using good living folk to accomplish awful things." He smiled, closed-lipped but sweet. "Like I told you, my mother loved to tell eerie stories. What I've heard makes me think there's something about possession that would transcend boundaries."

Put like that, David saw his reasoning. He also felt he should be blushing. "And if it doesn't work? If you get pulled back, like you did when you tried to go to Edinburgh with Paul?"

"Should have tried to jump into him instead of follow him."

Admiring the determined pluck with which he said it, David chuckled and thought for a moment. "I used kites as a metaphor," he said. When Alastair eyed him with some inquisitiveness, he elaborated. "I wondered about possession not so long ago. I thought perhaps it would be like holding a kite's string, but I didn't know which of us was which."

"A boat seems more obvious—and a little kinder— to me. I might be steering, sometimes, but mostly I'm just a passenger. It's still your vessel. Maybe that makes me different from the demons and ghosts in stories."

Smiling a bit, David traced his fingers along a smooth little stone that rested next to him. Then he said, "And I'll bring you back where you started after the deed is done."

Just in case, he thought. Something might go amiss for either of them, should he wander too long with another person's very being crammed alongside his own.

"That's wise, I should think."

"But we won't do any tattoos. I don't want them."

Alastair laughed, possibly most of all at his truculence. "Not even just a little one?"

Though Alastair was not serious, David felt he needed to prevaricate. "I hardly recognize myself these days. But a tattoo might be too daring, even for this new David."

Necromancy was one thing, and even he knew most people would balk at it. Regardless, he could not fathom embracing such a bold adornment. Some types of intrepidness were still not for him.

12

He was only passing by David's door when Theo heard his voice, muffled through the wood. Because Lennie was in the kitchen and not here upstairs, Theo wondered if David felt better and had roused himself to speak with Alastair or perhaps Benson. It had to be the prior. Theo caught no one else's tones, and especially not Benson's, which were distinct enough through either wood or thin air. He knocked, thinking to offer tea or something to drink. David carried on talking as though he hadn't heard.

Nudging the door open carefully, Theo said, "David?"

The scene was not entirely what he'd expected. David was abed under a blanket, not sitting up on the bed.

"Were you given to... habitually murdering?" David asked, his eyes shut.

Peering at him, Theo felt David could be dreaming. He never had spoken in his sleep in all the nights they'd spent together. Granted, they were not always sleeping, yet there'd been enough sleep for Theo to say with certainty he hadn't heard it. But David was now doing many things he'd never done. Rubbing shoulders with Paul Apollyon, running a public house, speaking with someone like Benson as though they were equals, talking to a—

Theo started when he noticed the man-shaped, opaque shadow lounging in the wingback chair by the unlit hearth. Afternoon sunlight made it obvious and stark enough. The illumination fell on the figure as much as it would fall on an ordinary person, but it underscored just how unfathomably deep its color was.

Talking to a ghost.

The very notion made Theo want to run and find Paul, tell him to go to sleep right this instant. It did not seem the shadowy man noticed him. At the least, it did not react. Perhaps it was just ignoring him. He was about to creep back out the door he'd rather boldly opened, but David's voice slowed his steps. "But you're talking of murder as though we're planning a menu."

Theo quite wanted to know who was the object of this conversation. That it was Alastair and David having it seemed clear. It might even be Alastair's proverbial unfinished business.

A great number of people seemed to natter on about ghosts having something left undone, including Benson. He was more prosaic and less dramatic in his suppositions than most, though. Said it could be something so simple as one's favorite scarf being given to the relative one had secretly most hated. This example seemed oddly specific, so much so that Tom had maintained it could not be made up. But no one wished to ask Benson outright.

In all of the traditional or popular ghost stories, it was always something rather more important than a scarf. One had been murdered and nobody knew the truth of it, or one had been denied the opportunity to marry one's love, or some such thing.

Theo waited, wanting to hear more.

He was not disappointed. In the natural amount of time it would take someone to reply, for David to then pause and formulate an answer, he mumbled, "My world felt that way, too. Eat, or be eaten. Although I wager your stakes were much more dire."

Father had always told Theo nosiness could not be rewarded. Despite this, Theo generally found it was rewarded with information. It was not his favorite kind of currency, but it might be his second favorite.

After another, longer span of moments passed, David said in a tone of ultimate resignation, "Fine. You can kill Ralph. If he doesn't die on his own, first."

Eyes widening, Theo did creep out of the room just as the shadow in the chair looked to be stretching his legs.

What he'd do with this information, he couldn't quite say. While he had never met Ralph and did not need to for his poor opinion of the man to remain, he suspected Lennie would not be happy for their stepfather to be murdered. Particularly if David might be planning it in the shadows with a specter.

Lennie had been subjected to so much manipulation that Theo couldn't imagine the withholding of something so irrevocable would go over well. Even if Ralph was the worst of men. The heart was complicated. It might *want* an end to something awful, while also desiring the least amount of hurt or conflict.

Mildly chewing at his lip as he thought, Theo reflected upon how steadfast morality could be juvenile without nuance. If it wouldn't greatly complicate things for David should he be caught, Theo might not mind Ralph's demise. He couldn't say what Lennie's thoughts on the subject were: they might indeed be malleable given their rather suspicious former occupation. However, his instincts said it would be David's clandestine involvement that hurt Lennie most of all, and experience did allow him to read others with some accuracy.

With a hushed grumble of recognition, he realized it could well be why Robbie had been seeing so much of David. Tom could not abide the sight of him after what Robbie had done to Paul and ignored the man when he came to Cromer.

Feigning ignorance was impressive given Robbie's size and bullish demeanor.

Theo, Tom, and Paul simply speculated that David might be trying to situate Robbie within better employment. Perhaps not with any of his own staff, seeing as Robbie had also broken into his home by Chapelfield Gardens. It might be odd for David to see him so frequently. But David was still quite connected to Norwich's various industries, so it would be easy for him to find something suited to Robbie. Perhaps within a warehouse or something similar.

Instead, Theo now wondered if Robbie was aware, or even the instigator, of a possible plan to murder his father.

On the one hand, some might argue death might be a kindness to a man so ill. Theo didn't know if he believed that was true. It seemed like a concept that could be so easily abused whenever one wished to justify killing.

But on the other hand, one could say such a killing was grimly just. From what Lennie had relayed to all of them, Ralph was not redeemable. His beliefs were erroneous and bigoted, while his desires were rooted in avarice.

The world really could be brighter without him. Lennie's most of all.

Questions and misgivings warred within his mind. Theo didn't particularly want to be the person who broke David's confidence. Once broken, he had the unnerving suspicion it might complicate matters for everyone remotely connected to David.

He frowned. Lennie very likely would not endorse this manner of help, no matter how poorly they'd been treated, and Theo had to admit that was an admirable quality. In addition, he couldn't ignore how strongly he felt that Lennie would interpret David's evasiveness as a betrayal of sorts.

"You look far too troubled for someone who has just pleasured me to within an inch of my life," said Tom.

Theo shook his head and slowly came back to rest along Tom's side. Always a fastidious creature, he'd left no evidence of the scintillating act he'd just performed. His jaw hurt very slightly. But he *was* tense, after all. "Why would you say so? Perhaps the light is too weak now for you to see me properly." He stroked at Tom's midriff, enjoying the play of muscles under warm skin.

Remembering when he'd eyed Tom through a gap in someone else's curtains, he smiled a little to think he was now ensconced in a very similar situation. One which he hadn't necessarily believed he'd experience. A bit of jealousy had even entered his mind at the time, and it wasn't that he thought he was above such a feeling. It just didn't always surface for him.

Eventually he did meet the man whose privacy

he'd so quietly invaded. Will turned out to be a friend of Tom's, the sort of friend whom one sometimes sought out for more carnal things. He was a sedate, good-humored, kind sort of person. Any sense of jealousy Theo possessed vanished when they were introduced. And if Will was disappointed to learn of Theo's role in Tom's life, he did not seem to ruminate upon it.

"I know what you look like when you're thinking something over." Tom trailed his fingers along Theo's arm. "Mind you, I'm not complaining about anything that just happened."

Neither, in fact, was Theo. Sex was all hunger between them, all joy, even if one or the other of them was rather preoccupied. The months they'd lived together hadn't dulled it, and he'd been prepared for such a thing. Everyone seemed to reference it, as much as anyone decent did reference pleasure.

It might happen, still, he supposed. If so, he would be eager to finesse his way to keeping Tom hungry. Or, he admitted, somewhat resentfully, to discovering what could if it was not him.

"I need to tell you something."

"This sounds familiar."

At that, Theo had to smile. "No, not to do with me. I overheard something today and I should like your thoughts on it."

"All right."

"But you have to promise not to tell a soul. Well, until we decide what to do."

"Heavens, now this sounds serious."

Tom wriggled himself into a sitting position and brought Theo closer to him. Happy to oblige, Theo leaned back and against his strong body. Carefully, Theo relayed what he'd heard David saying and the manner in which he said it. As he turned his head to see how Tom responded, his expressions roamed between confusion and disbelief.

When Theo finished, he looked more determined than anything else.

"We should tell Lennie," he declared.

Theo had been mildly afraid of such a declaration. "I don't know if the murder element will hurt them as much as the fact that David seems to be planning the event with a ghost, and possibly Lennie's stepbrother. Yet he hasn't told them."

The incredulity in Tom's eyes gave way to understanding, then ire. "That would account for why the bastard is underfoot more than I'd ever care to see him."

Hiding a smile, for they had really only seen Robbie one or two times, Theo said, "Yes, I thought so, too. I do feel he must know something."

"I wonder if he's the architect of the plan, then."

"Why not do it himself, alone? They live together. Robbie is his father's caretaker, same as David was for his father." When someone else said it, he felt it did not account for why David would be part of any said plan.

He eyed the candle burning lower on Tom's nightstand and waited for Tom to answer. He was in no rush to come to any conclusions, and the process was much better in his arms than it might be alone. Surrounded by the faint scent of Jicky, the light lavender and vanilla, and grounded by the feeling of his muscles and coiled sense of energy, Theo could let himself fret without fear of drifting too far into nerves.

"David's doing it for Lennie," said Tom.

Gazing at him, Theo gave a short and silent nod in reply. He agreed. "I think so. And I think it's possible he sees something of a shared struggle between them."

"I'd do it for you."

Blinking, rather struck by the assertion, Theo murmured, "I imagine that killing someone changes a person, no matter how noble the intention behind it."

"Then I'd be changed."

"I still don't think we should tell Lennie," Theo said quietly. "Think of the damage it could do them. They've often been manipulated, or most of their life hasn't *really* been within their control. I worry they wouldn't register this as very different." He could tell Tom disagreed from the way he stiffed slightly around him. The disapproval did not need to be said in as many words.

It was foreign, for they had not had deep arguments or disagreements.

At most, they'd irritated each other, which was not so stark of a feeling. Those situations were the same as what others faced. Perhaps someone tracked in sand and left the other to clean it up. Maybe Tom was too blunt for him, or Theo was too circumspect for Tom. Somebody might eat the last of the cheese without saying. If Tom was falling into a bit of a melancholic day, he was prone to snapping or sniping. Theo had a habit of letting him, which ultimately was constructive for neither of them.

Still, these were small and mundane, and never merited proper disapprobation.

Intuiting Tom felt more strongly about this, Theo still said, "I think they'd see it as a betrayal. I don't know if the death part would trouble them as much as David trying to accomplish it without them knowing."

"Then what do we do?"

"Nothing, perhaps." Saying something about it

was supposed to be helpful to his own emotional state —he'd felt he needed to share it with Tom. While there were things they didn't talk about because they each respected the other's privacy, this had felt different to him. Too big a thing to keep to himself. Theo hadn't expected it to solve the problem at hand; it was more David's than anybody else's. "Well, we don't tell Lennie."

"Why did you bother to tell me? Clearly, you could have kept your own opinion without saying anything."

Mystified by the coldness laced within his words, Theo said, "Why wouldn't I tell you?" He sighed. Tom was his confidante, and he hadn't meant to start a row. "I won't stop you from acting according to your conscience. If you truly want to say something, I understand why. But I'm concerned transparency may not be the best option."

Tom released him. Not roughly, but decidedly. "Respectfully, Theo, you might be a little long in the tooth to understand how we mortals think."

Surprised, and not just a little unhappy at the loss of contact, Theo peered at him. "What?"

"You think it's appropriate to let David go off and kill someone?"

Confused, Theo said, "No." He had not quite said what he thought of that. Tom had changed their positions before he could, disrupting his own flow of speech. "But you just *said* you'd do it for me."

"And I would, but I'd have the good sense not to get caught."

"So... you would do it for me and be clever enough to get away with it, but... nobody should do it?" Theo watched him curiously, trying to understand what emotions framed the contradiction.

"Yes."

"All right," said Theo, still perplexed and gleaning this present upset was scarce to do with David's potentially rogue and misguided morals.

"I'm also rough to begin with, aren't I?"

"What?" Never, in the entire time he'd known Tom, had Theo once associated him with the concept in any sense.

Huddled against the headboard, Tom huffed. Theo wanted to hold him, but refrained. "Never mind. I know what I just said. But it seems to me, if we know about it, we should stop him."

Even more baffled, Theo asked, "Can I finish my thought, please?"

Glowering, Tom nodded once.

"David should be intercepted." Theo carefully took Tom's hand from where he had it palm down, on the bed, and kissed the tip of his pointer finger. "I just don't think *we* should tell Lennie." He believed such a discussion should originate from David, or it would backfire. The knowledge alone wouldn't make Lennie feel better. "Perhaps I should have started with that."

"Oh."

Lightly, he kissed Tom's palm. "And you're not rough. I do think you could manage killing someone in defense. Maybe a couple of centuries ago, you could do it for your honor. But you're not rough."

That, he knew, was a holdover from Tom's younger years. David had only disparagingly referred to Tom before they'd become friends again. Theo was aware of how many times Tom must have heard something of the kind about himself. He was almost unearthly in his demeanor, if only because he did not play social games, and he always left one in little doubt of his vigor. Like his uncle, he was not a large man. But he bore muscle from his previous types of work.

The quiet intensity paired with physical prowess, as understated as it was, seemed to create the wrong impression that he was wild.

Some, like David had at his worst, might term it something like *rough.*

"Thank you," said Tom quietly.

Gently, Theo said, "What did you mean about me being long in the tooth?"

~

THE WORDS WOULDN'T COME, though not because of shame.

Once Tom let Theo speak a little more, he did feel a bit ashamed for snapping so. But mostly, he couldn't untangle what he felt, the *way* he had felt since seeing Theo in his other form.

Perhaps not his *truer* form, as Tom hadn't asked him if that were correct. There was nothing wrong with it, either. He was not under any impression that selkies were tantamount to devils, as he imagined some people might try to say. Fear of the forbidden or unknown was not the problem.

Seeing the physical change confirmed everything he had known in theory. Somehow, it was far more of a jolt than knowing, in the abstract, that Theo knew worlds he never would. Not just those under the water. He had experienced things well before Tom existed, and might continue to experience more after he was gone.

It couldn't be accounted for like a more ordinary difference in age, like the one between Alastair and Paul. *Or those between many women and their fiancés.*

Theo's perceptions, his perspectives, were things Tom could never access with much accuracy, unless they were about how Theo might view other people. In a sense, this was true of any other person. No one could know another as intimately as they wanted.

Yet, a selkie was not quite comparable to any other person of Tom's acquaintance. The space between what Tom was, and what Theo was, suddenly felt almost immeasurable.

Maybe you were naïve when you spoke to him in David's empty house. The distance hadn't seemed so vast, then. Now, he feared it. He was nervous that he might be too weak to cross it, or Theo might finally find him foolish or unworthy.

He should try to say some of this, as imperfectly as it might leave his tongue. Perfection and fear were the enemies of his expression.

Then, at least if he tried, he'd give Theo something to refute. Tom couldn't; the risk seemed too great in the moment. After enough time had passed for his question to fall flat, Tom imagined, Theo sighed.

With an air of understanding that Tom never thought he'd find in a partner, he said, "Never mind." Others might have pressed for more, pushed for what they wished to know. Theo always understood when to acquiesce, and Tom hoped it would not one day lead him to disappointment.

Theo inched forward and kissed him tenderly on the forehead. "For now, let's agree not to go to Lennie unless it becomes unavoidable. I don't know if that will happen, but it could. In the meantime, we shall look after David as best as we can, the sneaky fellow."

"What if we have to, I don't know, tie him up?" Tom found his voice with a bit of levity, and hated himself a little for it. How he so wished to be serious. "Keep him from doing something that might get him jailed for life." As he said it, though, he realized the courts would almost always favor Mr. Mills well over Mr. Campling.

"Then I pray you don't become too aroused by doing it." Theo smirked, and Tom knew he was in jest.

But the urge to claim his lips rather than jest in return was too strong. That, at least, Tom could enact.

13

———————

It had taken Paul a week of actively choosing to reopen himself to the ebb and flow that could be time—or madness—for there to be a change in his perceptions. He couldn't face the bustle of his daily life while he was trying to return to his former level of abilities. So he'd hidden himself away more than anybody was now used to, which roused concern.

Benson, though, seemed less troubled by this than he did ghosts, and ventured up to the landlord's flat with reasonable good cheer.

Four nights ago, now, Benson had asked while he lazed on the sofa, "Why did you not just *say* you'd given it all up?"

He'd wormed everything out of Paul at last, but Paul was also much less concerned with keeping the decision private after disclosing it to Tom and Theo.

"What would you have done?"

"Called it ridiculous."

"Anything else?" Paul swilled a bit of whisky.

"Said you should get it back."

"Why?"

"Forcing it away can't be good for you. Some urges are always meant to be followed. I don't know if God comes into things, but if you were made to do something, you should probably do it."

"What about you?"

Benson paused and took a long breath from his pipe, an ancient clay thing that had seen far better days. "Me?"

"Yes," Paul said. He straightened up as he sat in the wingback chair opposite the sofa. "Seems like you're not doing what you were made to do. You're just letting David do it."

Benson grunted, seeming peeved. But at least he answered. "Me and Timothy ran into some trouble with a ghost, years back."

"Your brother isn't a witch-hunter. Or a necromancer." He actively did not point out that Benson was using his brother's full name, which was not always his habit. Timothy apparently didn't enjoy pet names, but as a sibling was prone to do, Benson often employed his and called him Timmy.

"No. He never had the aptitude." That followed for Paul, as Edward had no magical talents. "But he'd often help me with strategy if I needed it, and he's a better reader than anybody David met at university. He never took to witchery; I never took to reading. It evened out."

"What happened?"

After a long and weighty span of quiet, Benson said, "A local girl was being haunted. Her mother knew our parents, and knew they were of a witchy persuasion. But they were getting on in years, by then, so Father said *I* should go see what all the fuss was about. Timothy came, too."

Finding it easy to be patient because this was the most personal information he'd ever received in one conversation, Paul said, "And?"

When Benson's eyes met his, Benson said curtly, "The spirit saw an opportunity. He got possessed." The three words conveyed enough strife, and Paul let them hang. While he considered asking for context, for depth, he didn't dare. It was more important to know anything, and asking might derail Benson.

He knew things must have turned out reasonably well in the end, for Timothy was still spry and of sound mind. He didn't angle to learn more, and instead moved to refill Benson's empty glass. "Thank you for telling me."

"I did say they'll use anybody as a puppet."

"I remember." Paul didn't suggest that he wouldn't mind being Alastair's puppet. It wouldn't fit the somber tenor of their conversation.

"Timothy came through it, but he never went near magic again. And he didn't even have any to begin with. His fear parted us for a number of years, and I can't blame him. But you?" said Benson, accepting the refreshed whisky with a small nod. "You need to get to seeing things, again."

Paul took the directive to heart. His efforts returned what he'd ignored for so long, and true to his experience as a younger man, the theme of things was rather banal.

His first premonition in years was to do with Mrs. Lloyd coming into money after a distant relative's death. But it was indeed a premonition. A victory. He was unsurprised it came through a dream, yet it had been long enough since his last experience that the whole experience felt feverish.

Paul had needed to remind himself they were lurid and sensory. Because he didn't wish to advertise the change to anybody, he simply did not say a word and carried on as he had been. If there was more lightness to his step, no one commented. That was just as well, for it all seemed tenuous enough. He didn't want to be congratulated before determining if he was actually once again on form as a seer.

The same night Mrs. Lloyd happily relayed that her cousin had left her an as-yet unknown sum and she was to find out the specifics at the weekend, Paul crept to bed with the keenest and sharpest of hopes. If *that* had come to pass, and surely if Benson had been supposing correctly when he mentioned the possibility—he usually did make irksomely correct suppositions for a man who wasn't a seer—Alastair could make use of Paul's dreaming state.

Alastair did not come the night Mrs. Lloyd announced her good news, or during the night after.

On the third, Paul retired, exhausted by the day's work. Less hopeful than he had been. Indeed, he was trying not to give up. He did not want to sink into that comfortable and deadened ache. Fate had woven unseen bonds between him and Alastair, and shown Paul life could be magical in its way. He wished to remember that above all else.

Nonetheless, his hope had dulled.

It was so like Alastair to make an entrance then, when Paul was really rather worn down and at a loss as to what would happen next. They'd met under those circumstances and Alastair possessed a flair for dramatics.

At first, Paul might have believed he'd simply sleepwalked to his own parlor and awoken into sleepy consciousness. But the light was different and there were fewer of his effects in the room. It looked newer than it had in years. When he looked out the window, he could see nothing but fog, diaphanous and luminous gray. Intriguingly, he still heard the promenade and sea beyond.

He was trying to peer through the fog when a voice murmured from behind him, "Been an age, angel."

He could have said a great many things, all of them soft and necessary. A more poetic man might have managed, and a sweeter man might have tried. What came out first was a level, quiet, "Took you long enough."

Paul now understood it had been his own truculence, his own grief, that had hindered the process, along with David's bewitchment. All the same, he could not help but default to the banter that had been so customary between him and Alastair, even though the tenor of Alastair's voice washed over him like a warm bath on a cold autumn evening.

"Well, *someone* proved very stubborn." There was a smile in the words. "I had to take the long way. But the very stubborn someone is so beautiful, it was an acceptable journey."

"I don't even know how I'm doing this," Paul admitted, his voice trembling only a little. "If you're dead and not of the future."

"Best not to question it too much, lest your mind make the walls dissolve into one of Dante's circles of hell."

Paul had to chuckle. "I don't want that."

"Sweet boy, you can turn around. I won't disappear if you look at me."

Secretly, Paul had been afraid of such a thing. "You might."

Footsteps, just as recognizable as his own, came closer and halted just nearby. Paul tensed, not from nerves, but from a longing so clear that it stunned him.

When Alastair spoke again, his words were warmth caressing Paul's ear. "It's all right. You can relax. I've been practicing."

"What the hell do you mean?"

"I've been using David's dreams to practice entering them. We've done one on the beach, we've done one in this Cambridge library I'd never have been able to visit otherwise... it's remarkable, and don't ask me how it works. I don't know. I don't know if anyone does."

"It *is* remarkable. Is that why he's stayed here, the sly thing?" From what Paul had understood, David had been feeling unwell and simply didn't wish to relocate. It mattered little, and Lennie, probably on David's behalf, was sneaking money into the till by way of payment. Paul was ignoring it, then putting it back in their wallet. "He's got a beautiful house not far from—"

"Paul, you really can face me. I'm not going anywhere."

Expelling a long breath, Paul decided to believe him. He half-turned and glanced up to meet Alastair's eyes. They hadn't changed; nothing about him had. He looked as he had on the night he'd died.

Paul, however, knew *he* looked different and hoped Alastair would not find fault in it. Vanity, perhaps. Quiet, gazing at him as though looking away would now cause him to disappear, Paul waited for his pronouncement. He thought age had been kind to his appearance and did not dwell upon it much.

But he had, naturally, changed since Alastair's death.

"Look at you," said Alastair. Nothing but love was

in the words, love and a little awe, and Paul smiled slowly.

"If I'm to believe everybody... well, two people in particular... you already *have* been looking at me."

"I always turn my back when you get dressed. When you bathe. When you relieve yourself, obviously." Alastair winked and Paul almost wept at the sight. "I'm still a gentleman."

"Always were." Paul wanted to reach out, to touch him, but his hands were fastened at his sides. After a span of seconds that felt like an eternity, he said, "Touch me?"

It seemed even Alastair was wary of what might transpire if they did try to touch, for he hesitated despite the eager spark in his expression. Then, finally, he brought fingertips to the very edge of Paul's cheekbone.

Paul's gasp was more of a shudder combined with a small, drawn breath; Alastair's gasp mingled with a gentle, quiet utterance of *fuck.*

"Wait, could we?" It left his lips before he could reconsider sounding like an overeager boy who had never slept the night with anyone. Paul should have blushed at the amount of need in his own question.

He didn't.

Appearing to give it the barest amount of consideration, Alastair said quickly, "The worst that might happen is... you wake up. I reckon."

"I thought you were worried about what my mind could do."

"Yes, if you start overthinking," said Alastair archly. "But I seem to recall fucking was one of the few things that kept you from overthinking."

Unable to argue with that, he wordlessly grabbed Alastair's hand—warm, solid, blissful—and pulled him to the bedroom, which thankfully did exist within the confines of his dream.

~

HIS NEXT VISION after seeing Mrs. Lloyd's good fortune left him perplexed.

For hours after waking, Paul wondered if his mind was simply confused—mixing his joy at seeing Alastair again with anxiety at the prospect that he might fade away once more.

On the other hand, the morning after he and Alastair slaked their lust in a dream, he'd also wondered if *it* had been a normal dream. In the end, he'd supposed not: his mind had not managed to recreate anything from Dante, or wake him up, or otherwise ruin any of the proceedings. Tom had to ask him three times if he was all right. Once, just after he rammed his thigh into the edge of the bar, and again when he dribbled hot tea down his chin and front. The third time, Paul had smudged someone's surname in the ledger to the point of illegibility.

Then he'd excused himself to see to the kitchen's stores.

But not before Benson passed him in the corridor and muttered, "You're positively glowing" in a manner that left very little doubt Benson knew what'd happened.

If it had just been because Paul was making obscene noises in his sleep, someone else would have overheard too.

It would be so like Benson to ferret out knowledge of an assignation within another plane of existence. If Alastair was speaking to him, there would be no avoiding the topic. Always a gentleman, but equally eager to show off his and Paul's love where he knew it was safe to do so, Alastair would likely demure. Tell Benson to fuck off in a good-natured fashion. Then bestow the truth upon him.

At present, two nights had passed since that happy night and Alastair had not returned. Though a glutton for him as he always was, Paul was content to trust he would come back when he could.

It was a startling change to how restless he had felt in Portobello, when he could not look at a grave. But now Paul knew how much Alastair had wished to be near him, too. The knowledge allayed most of his restlessness.

Last night, though, he had not dreamt of, or had, sex. He did not know the underlying truths of what had allowed them to reunite. If Benson knew enough to allude to it, it must have *happened* in some sense of the word, and not only in Paul's imagination.

His last dream had been awful. Paul had dreamt of Alastair in a dark, filthy, cheerless room with a man who had the look of one who'd been drastically ill and had aged beyond his years. The light, such as it was, allowed for little to be discerned beyond the two. The stranger, splayed on a bed under an old blanket. Alastair, looming above him like an angel of death, affixing a palm across the man's gaping, bloodless lips.

A struggle, minimal and borne of a human instinct to survive. Only on the stranger's part as his limbs twitched under the blanket and he struggled against the palm.

Alastair, who was the same age he appeared to be now, appeared less than troubled, almost content to watch and wait until the struggle ceased. He looked at home in the semidarkness, the sort that fell through windows during a late autumn afternoon or lingered as the sun rose in early winter. There were no candles to provide illumination.

Paul had never seen him this way, neither in life nor in a premonition.

He knew enough of Alastair's past to understand he'd been party to crimes and even deaths. From what he understood, most of the violence had been part of Alastair's younger years, driven by desperation and lack. Marriage had eventually tempered him. He found less risky means of surviving, for he said it would be unconscionable to imperil not only himself, but a woman and child as well.

He had a reputation, he'd explained. But that could cut both ways. It might keep people from him, and it might also motivate people to try to hurt him.

Paul always felt it was sad that Alastair did not seem to view himself as reason enough to seek more stability and safety. He'd needed others who depended on him, then he sought a more normal life. He did find both at The Shuck, or as they called it then, The Queen Anne.

Even knowing what he knew of Alastair's previous choices, Paul was unnerved to bear witness to what happened in that unfamiliar and dank room. He'd come awake gasping, unsettled, trying to make sense of the vivacity of smell, color, sound. All paired with the actions of a man whom he now knew was very much present in The Shuck, but who was also very much dead.

All of what he'd experienced before closing himself off from premonitions said something so lurid was bound to happen, and besides that, he never saw things that were of the past. But there could be no way a dream of such a subject conveyed a future event—

Alastair wasn't alive. He couldn't influence the future so directly.

In spite of knowing this, Paul was still unsure.

He only *thought* he knew it. His old wisdom of how his abilities worked was helpful, but some of it had been proven wrong. Or at the least, it had expanded.

Never had he experienced a visitation from a ghost in his sleep—and he could not decide if he was pleased or disappointed he still could not sense Alastair while he was awake. *You should be pleased. If you could, he would drive you to distraction.*

He'd puzzled all day over what last night's dream conveyed, what it might signify. Because things had changed so radically, he was no longer content to rely on what he had known to provide an explanation.

The ill stranger, he had never seen in his life. The sad bedroom, he had no knowledge of.

But Alastair, he knew as intimately as he could. He was as close to Alastair as he'd been allowed to get. That was what gave him such pause. Threads of a similar kind had always connected all of his premonitions to him.

Although it was tempting to try to rationalize the disturbing sight into the paradigm of a normal dream, Paul's reawakened instincts whispered it would not fit.

14

———

Knowing David was well now was not terribly comforting; Lennie wanted to know why he had been so ill in the first place. To that end, they'd pelted Benson with questions for a fortnight. Now he avoided them whenever possible. It was to his benefit that Lennie did not usually live in The Shuck, for if they had, he wouldn't have had a moment of privacy past those needed to relieve himself.

Lennie especially troubled him in the evenings. It was easy to corner him. Benson was almost tolerating it, even if he did scuttle away.

They'd asked David once, not so long ago, if he'd consider moving house to Cromer, and he may as well have done so. For some reason whose full rationale was known only to him, they'd resided in his Cromer house since the weekend after he seemed fully re-covered.

Today, almost two weeks later, Lennie had come to a conclusion and wished to know if they were correct.

Benson glowered at Lennie from his place in an old, far too overstuffed chair. He'd initially appeared to think he could avoid them by decamping to the common areas outside of the taproom. But they were all smaller and less busy, so it had the opposite effect of what he wanted.

"I've told you everything I know."

After he ate in the evenings, Lennie noticed Benson was generally slower and as docile as he could get.

"I highly doubt that." They reflected upon what someone like Robbie would do if he were faced with somebody who refused to speak freely, and admitted to themself they could not behave accordingly. "This is why you're so frightened of hauntings, isn't it? Illness. But surely witches can make you equally ill, and you've been a witch-hunter your whole life. You don't run from David."

Or anyone in the immediate vicinity, Lennie silently added. The Shuck was a locus of preternatural folk, almost as though she was one too.

Though they could accept they might never know much of anything about Benson, they would push him to reveal more about this particular subject. Between David's cheerful but sudden and firm decision to reside here, and their odd encounter with Robbie, they sensed something was underfoot.

They did not like being so near the edges of *something* and it made them restless.

A strange restlessness, actually, had settled on all of them. Theo did not quite meet their gaze in the manner they'd grown accustomed to, Tom seemed busier than ever—although that did make some sense, for Paul had been less present downstairs—and David was conducting all of his business as normally as possible, with the exception that he was no longer having his regular appointments in the office on Upper St. Giles.

When Lennie had offered to stay in Norwich themself, as would be customary for most kinds of managers if their employer resided away from the place of business, David had balked.

"I need you here," he'd said, all large blue eyes and near-sincerity. Something about the earnestness did not land correctly, leaving Lennie to try to piece together what David was thinking and not saying.

They had stayed, but they had not entirely believed him. At least it did not matter much where anyone was, as David's contacts and clients were proving as flexible as ever. One of the things about having wealth that Lennie would never understand was how malleable it made others. Even if one was not supplying those people with payment through bribery or more upright means, money seemed to convey a trustworthiness that extended to most areas of life.

If a man like Mr. Mills said he was presently based in Cromer, his clientele simply accepted it. Some of them even remembered his mother was from Overstrand and attributed his changed venue to a family affinity for the sea. From what Lennie had gleaned from David's diary, people were either willing to wait until he came back or come to Cromer for their business matters.

"I don't run from David because he's about as threatening as a dolly's little tea set."

"Perhaps he's far more threatening. He can do what you can't."

"He can do what I won't," came the acrid reply.

Lennie had explained the channeling to Benson. Well, the possession.

They'd even poorly relayed the Gaelic word Alastair had used, and Benson had nodded. All he'd said beyond the nod was that witch-hunters were not excluded from having other talents, which he'd mentioned before.

Lennie understood the witch-hunter designation to be almost like practicing within a religious sect, much like one could be Anglican or Catholic under the wider category of Christian. There might be philosophical differences between the two, but they were arguably more alike in a broad sense than they were disparate. Somewhere in their bloodlines, Benson's ancestors and David's had decided they were of the hunting ilk.

Maybe because being on the other side could mean torture and death, never mind a terrible afterlife far away from heaven.

Choice was, as far as Lennie could tell, the only thing really separating witches from the witch-hunters. David and Benson, in turn, had decided to turn their families' inclinations toward good ends.

They no longer hunted, but they did seem to protect, or try to do so.

"Fine. He does what you won't. Does it have something to do with how tired he was?"

"Yes."

"Is that why you won't do it?"

Lennie knew the aptitude had to be there. Benson had to be able to do it, or he would not be so knowledgeable or afraid. When one considered how long Lennie had known Benson, it was not a lengthy acquaintance. But it was an acquaintance of the sort that had deeply demonstrated how nervous Benson was around specters. He was even wary of Alastair, who had never been anything to him but a friend.

There had been no discernible reason to Lennie's untrained eye, until they'd seen how tired David was after letting Alastair use his body. They didn't know how it worked. Magic was fairly ineffable, so that didn't worry them. Neither were they religious, so the concept of hell was irrelevant. But it *had* worked and there were tangible effects upon David's body, consequences which were relevant to their interests.

Not for the first time since they'd met David, they silently thanked Mum for raising them as she had: with an unwavering belief in the preternatural, and with curiosity about things they could not explain. If she hadn't, Lennie imagined things would be much more unpleasant for them. They might be trying to make circumstances fit limiting and dogmatic ideas, which never ended well for anyone and generally led to malcontent.

"My reasons are mine," said Benson. "All *you* need to know is that if David chooses to embrace this aspect of witchery, being tired is normal. And you need to be careful."

"Me, specifically?"

"Yes."

They hadn't thought about it, given Alastair was not even visible to them unless it was under very specific conditions. Being careful didn't make sense because there was nothing to be afraid of, in their case. "I don't. Ghosts aren't my area of expertise."

"They don't need to be. It isn't a requirement for possession."

That sounded ominous, but Lennie wouldn't concede it did. "Well... I'm not worried about me."

Benson said, grudgingly, appearing to deliberate upon what he should or wanted to say, "It'll become easier for him."

That was not all Lennie needed to know, and they supposed fatigue was not the only thing that would happen. Whether Benson spoke with a bias that was his alone and therefore things were not so dire, or there were deeper consequences to David's explorations, they couldn't say. They suspected the prior was more likely to be true.

"I think you're biased."

"So what if I am?"

"You don't need to be so leery all the time."

"Can't tell me what to do."

They sighed. "Fine."

Benson changed the subject, seemingly finished with the matter. "Have you heard anything about your bitch of a father, lately?"

"He doesn't contact me, these days." Lennie did not say this was due to David furnishing rather a large sum to Robbie, who was in effect Ralph's caretaker. It seemed self-evident enough that David must have had a hand in their newfound peace.

"I said *about*, not from."

"I don't care if he lives or dies, so long as he's leaving me alone."

As soon as they said it, though, they were less convinced. Ralph still frightened them, and though they did not wish for it in any active way, his death would alleviate many of their fears. It didn't matter that they didn't know exactly what he could do in his state. They had seen him, after all, witnessed firsthand how feeble he was now.

Their heart could not integrate the changes to a man who'd once permeated almost every aspect of their life. All aspects, in fact, except for their own inner world, which they fiercely guarded from his influence.

Watching them closely, Benson said, "He seems closer to death's door, if I'm to believe David."

"He could be. When I last saw him, weeks ago,

now, he was almost unrecognizable. David hasn't even seen him—he just heard me recount it." Guiltily, they tamped down the thought that their first visit to Ralph had been under cover of darkness while David was sleeping. David knew only about the official visit they'd agreed upon with Robbie that same night.

"Heard he was confined to bed."

"If you'd told me that was how he'd end up when I was a child, I wouldn't have believed it."

"He's totally bedridden, your stepfather?" Paul's soft voice carried into Benson's corner, and he appeared bearing a cup of tea and a quizzical expression. Evenings usually saw him drifting about his establishment. Often, he served people from behind the bar, but it was equally likely he'd be tidying or catching a small moment of pause, like he was now.

Lennie inclined their head in a slight nod. "Yes, and he has been for some time. Robbie has a time keeping him in bed in the small hours, though."

With an unsettling amount of hesitation, because in Lennie's estimation, Paul was always the epitome of calm surety, he said, "I've been puzzling over a premonition, and I can't make sense of it."

"So glad you're having them again," said Benson, and Lennie snorted at the amount of smugness in his words.

Paul, however, seemed to allow the smugness to roll off himself like water on waxed cotton. He spoke to Lennie directly. "In it, Alastair kills a man in his bed."

~

WHAT COULD ONLY BE DESCRIBED as a muffled fracas reached Benson's little nook, and Paul grumbled in mild frustration. Tom was not the best person to handle bar scuffles; he was just as likely to eject anybody as he was to arbitrate a minor dispute usually brought about by a little too much beer.

Paul took a step in the direction from which he'd come. "You can follow me, Lennie."

"If you'd like," said Lennie, wariness written in their eyes.

Benson seemed content to be left alone with his thoughts, for he sprawled in the chair that was far too stuffed for its size. "I find I don't want any excess company."

"You'd not help, anyway." If Tom was likely to eject offenders for the smallest of infractions, Benson was likely to open bets upon who might win a tussle.

Lennie shadowed Paul as he doubled back to the taproom. When he arrived at the threshold, he saw nothing particularly out of place and met Tom's eyes from across the milling room. "What happened?" he called.

Theo, who was ferrying a pint glass partially full of water back to the bar, answered him. "What always happens? Maeve frightened us all by alighting not a set of curtains, this time, but Mr. Gates' hat, over there."

Shaking his head in resignation as Theo rejoined Tom, then served a young man several moments later, Paul murmured to Lennie, "I haven't the heart to ban her. She's a friend of Mrs. Lloyd's, and quite a lovely woman when she isn't losing control over her latent fire witchcraft." He led them to one of the tables closer to the far wall. Lennie was uncharacteristically silent. "A small case in point of why I wish we were all brought up as you were."

Peering at him, Lennie said, "In poverty?"

"No," said Paul, full of patience and affection for them, "by a mother who treated magic just the same as the weather."

"Oh." Although the syllable was calmer than their short question, as Lennie sat across from Paul, Paul noted their disquiet. He wondered if it had most to do with his own disclosure and slightly regretted bringing it up at all. Lennie's gaze drifted to the beams above their heads, old things that had seen far more than any of the people who frequented The Shuck ever would. Lennie's eyes rested on the sigils Benson had inscribed over the doorframe, then on the ones closer to the bar.

"Lennie?"

"I've seen this. Lots of times."

Paul did not have to be told more than that to understand their meaning. "How?"

He was only curious about the specifics because he'd never actually encountered another seer besides Lennie, and even if he felt the same protective warmth toward them as he did toward Tom, he and Lennie were peers in that regard.

He suspected they could teach each other, or at least relate to each other's experiences.

"I've dreamt of it, only I don't hear anything. Well, it's so muffled. But you speak to me and..." they took a deep breath. "It's important, if I've had the dream so many times." Then they added, "Well, it's important to me or somebody near me."

"Has this happened to you before? A repeating dream."

They smiled a little and shrugged. "Twice. Once when I was very little, and it was just about a pretty silver horse I got to meet one morning. His owner let me pet him." Paul chuckled. "The second time, I was seventeen and kept dreaming of Robbie slicing up his palm in a fight. The fight didn't much matter, but the cut got infected and Ralph was angry he needed to see a real doctor for it. He might have lost the hand if he hadn't, honestly."

Doctors cost money, Paul thought, full of disdain for such a parent. "And now, you've had this one. This premonition."

"The only thing that changes is the lighting and the number of people around us. But it's you, dressed as you are now, looking as you do now, speaking to me. I recognized you the second David brought me here because of it."

With compassion, Paul tried to assess how they were feeling and how much he should divulge. Hearing this, he suspected his own premonition's veracity. Although the future did not always play out so linearly, in his own experience of seeing things that would come to pass, what he saw was often literal and exact.

The seers in myths might see things symbolically and need to tease out their meanings to apply them. He had not.

It didn't mean it was impossible, as this season of his life seemed to be all about the impossible. But he was old and wise enough not to force any conclusions, which was why he wanted to speak to Lennie now.

Gently, he said, "Ralph is that ill, then." It was not a question, and briefly, he described what the man he'd seen looked like in his mind's eye.

"That's him," said Lennie with distaste. "And his room."

Speaking to another person who shared his talents was refreshing.

There was no hesitation or doubt on Lennie's part,

and there were no confused questions about what Paul meant or if he had *truly* seen what he had seen. "But what I can't understand is why I would see Alastair there. I have been wrestling with the idea that perhaps it *was* only a dream—after all, I'm only a man." He chuckled a little. "I do have ordinary dreams, and have had far more of them in recent years. When I sleep deeply enough, anyway."

"So," said Lennie, with a small smile, "since your return from Edinburgh, you've been... opening yourself back up to..."

"Time? Magic? None of us know what to call it, do we?"

They nodded, appearing rather lost in thought. This was not a particularly raucous night in the taproom, not by Paul's measure and even in spite of Maeve setting Mr. Gates' hat on fire. But for most people, being pensive amidst the clamor would prove difficult.

Not so, for Lennie. Paul could almost see their mind working, sorting through things they were not voicing.

When Lennie spoke again, Paul had consumed half his tepid cup of tea. "I haven't told anyone but Benson this."

"You don't have to tell me, whatever it is," Paul said.

"I think I need to."

"Then, do."

"Alastair can possess David. It doesn't sound pretty, put like that. I suppose the kinder way of putting it is, David can channel him. Benson says it is something he *won't* do—and seeing as David was weak as a new kitten after, I can't blame him."

It was true that David had been, of late, subdued

and wan. Paul tried to square Lennie's revelation with Alastair's newfound intensity, his ability to inhabit dreams, one which Paul had attributed largely to himself. Perhaps it was all of the circumstances and parties combined at the right time: a seer who was again embracing his powers, and a ghost who had a person uniquely suited to facilitating his communication.

He rubbed at his temples. Whatever the reasons for all the change, he could not pretend he'd been happier when he and Alastair were so keenly separated. But David might be opening himself up to something he was unprepared for if he was serving as a vessel for the dead. Benson certainly seemed to imply it, and Paul wouldn't soon forget what he'd divulged about his brother.

Without knowing precisely what had transpired, Paul knew it impacted Benson immeasurably. It must have been brutal or at the very least, exhausting. Being neither devout nor especially afraid of the occult, Paul had no ethical or moral stance on necromancy. He'd also had no personal experience with it, for ill or good.

Mostly, he just surmised it must be intense for the practitioners, same as any other witchery, and it might yield rather dire results.

If a considerate ghost like Alastair could possess David—or, as with Timothy, anyone without magical abilities—so could a malicious ghost.

Paul didn't believe Benson's revelation was his to share with Lennie, so he held his tongue on the matter. Clearly, however, more risks were involved than he'd previously thought. "I don't see why it might lead to me seeing Alastair in Ralph's room, but thank you for telling me."

The thought of Alastair joining forces with David

was also immensely amusing, as they were such different men. He would have to ask Alastair about it.

Sounding hesitant, Lennie said, "I think David is keeping something from me. It might have to do with Robbie."

There was no love lost between himself and Robbie, but Paul endeavored to sound as neutral as he could. "What makes you say so?"

"Over a fortnight ago, when Robbie was here, I asked him why he and David were speaking so much." Lennie worried at their lower lip with their teeth. "I'd thought... employment, perhaps. David might be helping him find a situation. I know David despises him, but... David is a good man."

"What else?" Carefully, Paul gave Lennie a verbal nudge.

"He got cagey. Finally he said something like... David's doing it for me. I still don't even know what *it* is."

Then an answer lurked in Paul's mind, one that he was not very afraid of himself. But he knew Lennie wouldn't like it. "And Alastair is doing it for me. Well, for you and David, but..." In a fashion, it was for him. Alastair wouldn't stand for anyone close to him being hurt, and Paul knew he had an approach to justice that might border more on most people's idea of vengeance.

Ralph was a terrible man who actively hurt others, and secondly, his son had threatened Paul on the other end of a knife. Alastair would stand for neither of those things.

"What're you understanding that I'm not?" With a flash of the distrust that they seemed to be learning to shed, but that hadn't left them entirely, Lennie scowled.

Calmly, Paul asked, endeavoring to cushion Lennie as much as he could from the realities, "Where is David, now?"

"He was at home," said Lennie. "He's needed more time to himself, what with everything—"

Carefully, Paul stood and attempted not to look either too concerned or too intrigued. One might alarm Lennie; the other wasn't an appropriate response to his suspicions. But Paul had never been a staid man, or one content to just allow life to happen to him, and he could not help but be somewhat attracted to trouble.

"Come with me," he said. "We'll start there."

15

———

David *should* have been at home, but the house was empty and quiet. All Lennie heard were faint noises from outside; no staff were on hand and no faint, human noises echoed from downstairs. While Lennie appreciated Paul's serenity, for it kept them from shouting at nobody, it didn't lull them into thinking anything more pleasant.

They didn't want to think what they did, less because they wanted Ralph to live and more because David had kept something from them. If they contemplated the matter, and left aside Mum's better nature while embracing their own, they could admit that they felt no sadness or indignation at the idea of Ralph dying a little more quickly than nature might allow.

But in essence, David had lied to them. Even if it wasn't an active lie, he'd made a decision—quite a big one, from anyone's perspective—that did impact them. Lennie's younger years were too saturated with more pernicious deceits of the same kind. Their heart could not quite distinguish between what David wanted to do and what others had done to far worse ends.

In the end, David loved them. They knew this because it was infused in his look and touch. Forgiving him would happen.

It already has, they admitted. But they would allow the anger to coexist alongside the knowledge that this was someone they wanted to spend years with, whose hair they wanted to see fade to silver.

Between Paul's odd premonition and David's ability to commune with the dead, as well as Robbie scuttling about, it seemed there could be only one thing David intended to do. If he was indeed home, he could be intercepted before he tried. But Lennie worried he might be given to taking an abrupt action.

It was something about what Paul had seen so soon, and the manner in which it had been represented.

They thought back to David's clear, if stifled, rage in Paul's flat the night Robbie had slipped into The Shuck with a knife and desperation. They'd known he disagreed with their gentler approach then, and perhaps they could have tried to explain their reasoning just a little more.

It was not weakness or acceptance of poor behavior; it was self-preservation. They couldn't have a life with David while they were also living just as Ralph had encouraged them to—ruthlessly.

In short, they couldn't see how to be the person they wished to be and still aggressively interact with either Ralph or Robbie. The latter couldn't be part of their life or it would sour.

However, it seemed David had possessed the opposite line of thought. He had embraced a level of ruthlessness, but it was borne of love. Really, thought Lennie, it had to have been. He'd been so horrified to learn of Ralph's words and actions toward Lennie, and by then, Lennie had already seen sparks of adoration in his eyes.

When Lennie and Paul entered the bedroom, there was a brief note on the bedside table Lennie used. It was written in David's hand.

Gone out for a bit, be home soon—D

Lennie supposed it would be too lucky for the note to explain anything in more detail; David was too clever to put into writing anything to the effect of, *I'm just off murdering your stepfather so he never troubles you again, so do put the kettle on for yourself and please don't wait up for me.*

Sighing, suffused with rage and love, Lennie put the scrap of paper back where they'd found it. Then they glanced at Paul, who'd quietly accompanied them to the room. "I suppose he could be doing something perfectly innocent."

"Do you actually believe that, or do you wish to believe it?"

The timing would not allow for true belief. Within Robbie's plaintive words and Paul's dream, Lennie could not quite find the space to think David had merely gone down the pub—besides, which pub would he favor these days if not The Shuck—or a leisurely evening stroll along the prom.

"I would love to believe it," said Lennie.

"Well, we can return to The Shuck and ask Benson if Alastair is there. That'll be quicker than waiting for me to fall asleep, at any rate." After what Lennie presumed was an attempt at humor, Paul added, "And if he isn't, as much as I don't want to say this, perhaps we'll know where they both have gone."

Lennie appreciated the tact and the manner in

which Paul was attempting not to alarm them. But as the fateful discussion in the taproom had at last unfolded, they'd seen comprehension spark in his face.

Then, they realized within almost the same instant what he had also known. If he saw Alastair committing violence, it was because in some sense, Alastair would.

On occasion, Mum had remarked that visions might not be exactly legible. Sometimes they made the most sense after the event had come to pass. Part of her art, she said, was learning how to untangle them before that moment. Paul seemed different from her in the sense that his own premonitions were generally less symbolic. Lennie had this in common with him.

But because of Mum, Lennie knew it was possible for someone to see things that might not be a literal reflection or translation of what came to pass.

"All right."

Deflated, they kept trying to retrace every moment of privacy they'd had with David, wondering precisely how long he'd been kindling the desire to do away with Ralph. When they looked for it, his fury was a lingering thread, hot and repressed. In the moments just after he'd come upstairs after Robbie held Paul and Lennie at knifepoint, David had not understood Lennie's more merciful outlook. Other tells were present, too, all of them saying quite clearly that David could not tolerate injustices toward Lennie as well as Lennie themself might.

Tolerating them doesn't mean I condone them.

They were all but silent on the walk back to The Shuck, and silent still when Paul brushed their arm affectionately before he went off to find Benson.

In all the activity of the last several weeks, it had

been logical and sensible to attribute David's slight, almost imperceptible edge of distance from them to everything else: Paul's drunken flight to Edinburgh to do naught more than come home days later, having hit a near-stranger. Keeping The Shuck open while the three people most suited to running it were away. David, meanwhile, was communing with a ghost, and rather ill because of it. Alastair hadn't intended that and Lennie didn't take issue with him for it, but David was more haggard than he usually was.

On balance, there had been too much going on for Lennie to pull him aside and ask if everything was all right, or what the relationship between them both was meant to be. In some sense, Lennie was too thankful they fit with David to retain much guardedness when it came to matters of the heart.

They did not begrudge Paul the journey, especially considering he'd returned from it with new self-knowledge. Life, as it could so often do, had worked in a rather curious and circular way.

They did not even judge themself much for failing to see what David had obscured from them. They loved him, and that much was not up for scrutiny. Love could temper one's sharpness, and because it could, hopefully the object of one's affections was a decent person. David was decent, and so attuned to injustices that it might be his undoing. In concept, this particular killing did not trouble Lennie as much as it should. When they considered David's lack of pre-paredness for it, his lack of exposure to things like violence, it was a laughable idea that he'd manage.

Lennie had never been party to murder or torture; they did not have the stomach for either. Thankfully, their work as a pickpocket had not required such dubious fortitude. But brutality always lingered just beyond their own sphere of the demimonde. They heard tell of it from time to time. It was still far more often than anyone from the Mills' position in society might have heard about it.

Murders were generally much more mundane than the newspapers made them seem. For every scenario like the so-called Ripper's senseless murders of women, which Lennie remembered captivating anyone who read newspapers and magazines, there was another that was much more quietly accomplished.

Lingering in the foyer, Lennie stifled a noise of impatience.

They *should* be concerned about what David wished to do, and less hurt that he had lied to them. But the fact of the matter was, their sense of betrayal was more piqued than their sense of morality.

After all, when they'd briefly wondered if Robbie might be convinced to abandon his father, the result of such a choice would be no different. Ralph could not fend for himself in even the way an older child might. Imperfectly, just enough to survive.

Lennie could not be angry with David for desiring the same thing that their heart had whispered, if just for a moment. There was nothing redeemable about Ralph, no shred of something decent to grasp. No one would miss him, no one would mourn him. Except for Robbie, who might not do it much anyway.

But whenever people started deciding who had the right to live and die, things seemed to go mad.

Still, there it was: Lennie was far more wounded David had not confided in them. They couldn't pretend they were above wishing death upon Ralph. Theirs had just been fleeting, and more passive.

"Hello."

Lennie blinked. Tom stood in front of them, watching them with concern. "Did you know?" Rapidly, they needed to know nobody else but a ghost knew what had been in David's heart. Ghosts didn't have an allegiance to the living.

If Alastair did, it was clear where his was tied. Not to Lennie. They could, in large part, excuse him.

Robbie knew. He must have.

They stifled a growl and peered intently at Tom.

If Tom had known, it would redouble their hurt. Tom and David had shared such formative experiences that Lennie sometimes wondered if they could ever mean as much to David. It was an infantile thought and most days, it registered as such. It did not, now.

"No, but—"

"But?" Lennie went right up to him and glowered.

"Theo, when David was sleeping, overheard half of a conversation with Alastair."

"When?" They bit out the word.

"Not so long ago." Tom stood his ground and only eyed them with what seemed to be more concern. "Not long enough for you to look so overset. David said something along the lines of, 'You can kill Ralph' if he didn't die of natural causes."

"How did Theo *know* it wasn't nonsense?"

"There was a shadow in the chair opposite the bed. Even Theo could see it."

That seemed like a good enough indication of David's conversational partner, and Lennie sighed before bowing their head slightly. They were almost of a height with Tom and eyed his chest. He wore an oxblood jumper today, one that looked exceedingly soft.

Speaking to the span of chest they were looking at, Lennie said, "I didn't ask him to do this."

"I know."

"Why is he doing it? You've known him longer than me." Furious tears blurred the sight of Tom's jumper, the lines of his body under the cloth. "You know him better than me."

"He's never spoken to me about it," came the soft reply. "I can't say for sure. But... love. I should think. He's trying to protect you, and this... would be a way to do it. And Alastair... well, he's wise enough to know, I'm sure, that Paul doesn't need to be protected. Anyway, it was your stepbrother who crossed Paul, not your stepfather. But I'm not given to believe Alastair likes bullies, and Ralph is certainly a bully—"

Tom must have halted himself upon seeing Lennie dissolve into crying.

They would have stopped talking if someone started to sob in front of them, if only because they wouldn't know what to do about it.

The very idea of being so valued, of anyone wanting to protect them so viciously, was so strong as to induce the reaction when someone else said it.

It was equally surprising when instead of pressing on or making a demure excuse to go away, Tom enveloped them in an embrace. They clung to him as one might cling to a bit of driftwood while being dragged out to sea, taking a few moments to compose their thoughts. Somewhere in the back of their mind, they told themself that Tom was an incredibly attractive person going out of his way to make sure they were not so overset. It was that thought which grounded them enough to chuckle.

With a hiccup, they said, "Thank you."

Then Tom released them gently and stepped back

slightly. "Whatever he's doing, it's nobly done. Misguidedly done, but nobly."

Lennie nodded, wiping their nose on their sleeve and looking, they imagined, a right mess doing it.

"You also deserve him."

That, they were less certain of.

Tom seemed to pounce on their indecision. "Somebody who feels so strongly that you should be safe, and... not blackmailed? Not shadowed whenever some madman acts on the whim to pressure you? Not insulted, degraded?" He smiled. "I assure you, you deserve it. You deserve even more than one person who feels that way about you, and you've found a handful of them. Better late than never, eh?"

"He's gone," Paul announced to the foyer while he reentered it, speaking as though he were a king about to hold court. Lennie had expected for him to say as much. Yet, the words set something in motion they would rather not have had to confront. "Which means we should perhaps consider going to Norwich directly to see what our unlikely pair is up to."

16

Norwich

Uncomfortable was the best word David could apply to the experience of transporting another soul in his person. *Ridiculous* was the second best.

When he quieted his own mind, he found Alastair became the voice in his head.

"We should have practiced this," David mumbled. "My carrying you, I mean to say. Obviously, we can't precisely practice a..." he lowered his voice. "Murder."

If we had, I think you would have lost your nerve.

This, David might not get used to as long as he lived. He had a colorful inner life, so the sensation of someone else occupying the same space as his own thoughts and monologue, such as it was, was almost too much. He'd also come to the conclusion that actually, he did not always think in words so much as with pictures and feelings. The presence of so many extra sentences was a little jarring.

He decided, though it might make him appear mad, to imagine Alastair outside of himself and walking alongside him. If he saw anyone he knew, he would claim to be practicing a speech. "I wouldn't have lost my nerve."

I can tell you're not happy about this.

"Of course I'm not. I'm not a selkie. What right do I have to start a relationship with a secret?"

Well, you're also not exactly relishing it, either.

David hurried past Jarrolds and thought longingly of tea and a glorious wander unburdened by Alastair's spirit or the knowledge they were about to do something so final. "No, not at all. But I can't abide the thought of the man lingering and deciding to make Lennie's life a living hell. My father lived for years after he fell ill. I was lucky. He became... not more pleasant, but... the last several, he was oddly..." David tried to find the correct term. "Docile."

This doesn't seem to be about your father.

"It isn't." When he was painfully honest with himself, it was about the glaring and impactful sense that if he did not rid the world of Ralph, Ralph would continue to make the world smaller for Lennie.

He was sure Alastair could sense this, being so intimately entwined with him as he was.

I know your heart about as well as you do. Better, maybe, on account of being an outsider. There's not a selfish motive here.

That was little comfort. "So, my plan, after we're through, is to pretend he simply... died."

It's what I would do.

"Have you done something like this?"

No, not specifically. But the cards are all in the right place, aren't they? He's ill; he's old.

David worried this did beg the question of why he was not just waiting for Ralph to die of his own accord. The answer in that case *was* about his father, as it could be found in what he'd said moments prior.

They might need to wait years; David did not have the fortitude to do so.

In addition, Robbie seemed capricious enough to decide once again to become more loyal to Ralph, but David needed to remind himself that it was not caprice. Ralph had conditioned both of the children under his care to act according to his will. So, in some senses, Robbie could not be entirely blamed for his inclinations.

Thankful that Alastair fell silent as they wandered closer to the Camplings' home, David tried to quiet his own nerves. He had the address from Robbie, although Robbie received his post from a pub on Elm Hill where he had been a man of all work, and not where he lived.

The house itself was in a rundown part of the city David did not generally find himself near. As he approached, his heart grew heavier.

Lennie had come from these circumstances.

Any comfort to be had must have departed when their mother died, and yet Lennie remained here for far longer than they'd wanted. He did not have a particular knowledge of poverty past understanding how very privileged he was, but David knew living with Ralph for so long, without their mother, had to have been a struggle for more reasons than lack of money.

Lennie was so curious and quick and sweet; the atmosphere around Ralph must have been stifling for them. Never mind anything about their identity and the issues Ralph took with it. Any good person would have been demoralized. Then, to have that paired with the daily maligning, the put-downs, the threats, *she she she*...

David pursed his lips against a wave of his own anger.

Steady on, Mr. Mills, came Alastair's voice, and David imagined Alastair slipping a smile in his direction.

It made him feel a little better.

The nearby Wensum brought with it an unpleasant sense of humidity. These houses had not been properly tended to for some years, which led to damp and rot. Both had wet, musty scents that lingered heavy in David's nose.

Before Alastair could ask if he was ready, David knocked on the door, having the unpleasant sensation that several pairs of eyes were on his back. Perhaps they were and folk watched from behind their flimsy curtains. He was certain he looked out of place, and it was still light enough, so he was sure he stood out.

Robbie answered the door. Shock was legible in his slack mouth. By contrast, his blue eyes were dull and deadened, as though he had not slept for a few days.

He took a moment, seemingly to gather his thoughts.

Then, after a breath, he murmured, "You're too late."

Alastair answered for David, as the three words momentarily robbed him of his own ability to respond. "He's dead?"

If Robbie thought it was bizarre that Edinburgh's syllables exited David's mouth, he did not say. Perhaps he did not notice. "Took a great gasp at noon and didn't let it back out."

David found his own voice again. "He's in there, now?"

'Course he is, David. Alastair was not unkind about it, but there was a little amusement in his tone, if David had his guess.

Nobody would rush to take the body; it was in the wrong part of Norwich, to start. Beyond that, if Ralph had any reputation at all, it must not be a good one.

With a hollowness David had not seen him exhibit before, Robbie shrugged. "I've sent word that he's gone. Someone will come." It was half-past one.

David knew the decent thing would be to invite Robbie to come away. It might be unorthodox to leave one's father's body alone in a house, but Ralph and Robbie's relationship had not been warm and loving. Alternatively, David could offer to sit with Robbie, to remain with him until the body was collected.

He offered neither option.

This had never been in service of Robbie, and David did not consider himself altruistic enough to stomach sitting near a corpse in a dirty home that had witnessed more misery than smiles. As the knowledge that Ralph was dead percolated for David, he knew he didn't even need to see for himself. Robbie, whom he was sure was not the most honest of men, was not lying—the shock was too real to be feigned and there would be little reason for deceit.

He swallowed, nodded once, and said, "Right. That's that finished, then."

Without any words of sympathy or counsel, he simply gazed at Robbie and turned to go. He needed to be somewhere familiar and gather his thoughts, since he was presently home to two sets of them.

As he turned his back, Robbie said weakly, "You'll be wanting your money back, I imagine?"

David took a step forward, but he shook his head and said, "You need it more than me." The last thing he wanted back were the funds he'd allocated to Ralph in the hope it might buy Lennie peace.

With nothing more to do there and filled with a

curious sense of deflated purpose, he set off for his own house. He was well aware it would be finer than anything Ralph Campling had possessed in his lack-luster and wasted life.

Anything, David thought, but Lennie. And they weren't a possession, anyway.

PAUL AND LENNIE arrived by late afternoon. The windows were open as Lennie quickly approached the house. It seemed odd, given Robbie had rarely opened them of his own accord. He'd never been concerned with a cross-breeze or ventilation. Paul, quiet at their side, seemed to keep pace with them easily. What he lacked in height he made up for in sure-footedness.

Lennie didn't knock. Instead, they called quietly through one of the small windows, "Robbie?"

When there was no answer, they entered through the unlocked front door, Paul still more silent than the only ghost they'd ever met. It took a few moments for Lennie's eyes to adjust to the dimness, as ever; Robbie sat in a chair that was too small for him by the head of Ralph's bed.

Everything was as Lennie had last seen it, perhaps dirtier. They stepped carefully toward their step-brother, just as thankful as they had been before that Ralph was neither shouting nor passing snide remarks.

"You don't have to be so quiet, Lennie," said Robbie.

"What do you mean?"

"You can't agitate him any longer."

"What?" They kept coming closer, not that there

was much more space to cover. Paul reached over and rested a hand on their shoulder.

But Lennie crept nearer, drawn like a moth by the single candle burning on the table used for everything from eating, to folding the washing, to doing school exercises.

The latter only completed until Ralph decided neither of the children in his care were good enough for school.

"He's gone."

Alarmed, Lennie said, "Has David been here?"

"Not in the way you fear, no."

"Right." It was difficult for Lennie not to sound disappointed. They did not need to clarify with Robbie, for there could be no other reason they and Mr. Apollyon had come here together. Robbie knew it. "You were in on it."

"In on it," said Robbie, "since the morning I woke up in that pub's cellar with your man looming over me like some ghost."

Somewhere very close, Paul cleared his throat. But Lennie was thinking back to the night Robbie had accosted them, using the blade of his knife to get what he wanted.

"He didn't kill Ralph."

"No. *Ralph* took a breath and never let it out. But your David was here," said Robbie, his eyes still on Ralph. "He was here, for a moment."

Lennie wished they could spare more energy for Robbie's grief, as complex as it might be. He sounded numb and nonsensical, but they were not naive enough to believe he would remain so. No correct way could exist for grieving a man who'd made life something of a living hell, even if at times he had been slightly more lenient to Robbie. Those incrementally sweeter times had never lasted.

Neither of them could ever guess how long Ralph's favor would hold, regardless of who fleetingly benefitted from it.

Paul's hand was not gripping them too tightly, though Lennie gathered from its firmness that he was trying to stay them in a tacit manner. But it would not bother them to see the lifeless face of the man who'd made them question all that they were. Who'd taken all the energy Mum possessed, and squandered it.

They took a quiet breath through their mouth, reluctant to smell anything the room embodied.

Before, Ralph was asleep when last they saw him, his face relaxed and slack in the way anyone's was while they slept. His illness had not been kind to him, but slumber had softened its visible impact.

Not so with death. He was as drawn and taut as one of the stone effigies in the Cathedral not far from here, his face as grim as one of the medieval men whom Lennie had liked to stare at whenever they visited.

They glanced at Robbie. "Do you want us to stay?"

Mute, he shrugged, his eyes not leaving his father's face.

It wasn't too late at all for grim business to be conducted, so Lennie asked, "Is someone coming for him?"

There would be no wake; they didn't even need to ask. There hadn't been one for Mum, and Robbie hadn't been raised with them as a custom.

Still silent, Robbie nodded. Lennie guessed he had sent a neighbor to relay the news; nobody liked Ralph, but there were those who'd felt sorry for young

Robbie and Lennie. Some of them still resided exactly where they'd been all of Lennie's life.

In fact, Lennie would not be surprised if one of them brought Robbie something to eat as the sun set.

After a moment, they said, "All right."

They thought to ask if Robbie had finally snapped. If this was covert patricide despite what he said about Ralph's breathing.

Upon thinking of it, an ember of anger flared into a small flame when they considered Robbie's part in David's planning.

Perhaps, a ghoulish part of them wished to know, Robbie had taken things into his own hands?

No, Robbie didn't have the teeth to imagine it. Not the boy who'd sobbed on Lennie in their shared little bed after his father told him men were not afraid of the dark. Lennie had no doubt that Robbie could be brutal when he needed to be, that he'd demonstrated his willingness to be if it were that or be brutalized himself. He had never turned the ability toward his father, who'd encouraged it all along. They sighed.

Thinking it through, they suspected David might go home if he'd already come here and found himself thwarted.

Especially if he were carrying Alastair the way a child rode upon their favorite relation's shoulders, he would likely be exhausted.

Can he just let him go?

Would Alastair just get dragged back to The Shuck by forces unseen, if so? At the moment, while they'd never tell Paul, who still lingered near them, Lennie did not much care what would happen to Alastair in such a situation.

"Come to David's if you find you can't be alone,"

said Lennie to their stepbrother. "I expect we'll be there for a little bit."

Still, he did not look at them, but his face softened into a slight smile. "If I do, I'll knock on the door, all respectable-like."

"Good. I expect decent manners," said Lennie.

They glanced at Paul, whom they fancied was watching them with respect more than trepidation.

To be fair, Lennie didn't know how they felt. It would have to be examined later. But they could not be too harsh with Robbie. They just knew they'd spent enough time in this room and would never return to it. The air was heavy, and a sensation like they were slightly drunk had left their face almost numb.

"Can we..." Lennie trailed off; they nodded vaguely toward the door.

Paul released his light grip on their sleeve and murmured, "Of course we can."

Without exchanging any more words with Robbie —Lennie did not believe in platitudes, especially for the despicable dead—they quit the room and breathed more deeply when they reached the street outside. They'd never fainted and didn't wish to start now, but imagined this was how it felt before one did. The influence of knowing Ralph was gone and no longer able to torment them was, apparently, potent.

Well, they'd resent him more if even the stark relief itself instigated a faint. Lennie did not swoon.

Seeming to sense their physical difficulties, Paul was at their elbow, quick and silent as a cat. "If we walk a little to one of the main roads, we can hail a cab."

He touched them only minimally, one arm around their waist loosely, one palm resting carefully on their arm. The contact was appreciated as much as the consideration—though Lennie understood why Paul would be reticent, given they'd just walked out of their stepfather's home.

Paul's presence had never caused them any disquiet, though. He'd been nothing but respectful, always.

Lennie shook their head. "A walk will do me good."

17

David knew he surprised Mrs. Greaves and Ellie, and certainly Musgrave, who was always vigilant and on a knife's edge regardless of how calm life was. It was a consequence of prior military service, one that the Mills had accepted with varying degrees of grace. Father saw it as a weak but understandable effect of having been in combat, and had employed Musgrave as an act of charity. David, however, was actually rather fond of the man.

In the end, they were all pleased to see him, and surprised to hear David decline a bath because he loved baths. David did not have the heart to explain that, at present, he felt it would be strange to bathe.

Dinner was an equally strange affair, an array of cold plates gathered together due to the short notice. But at least he was not naked in a bath. The thought of being naked around Alastair touched a nerve he hadn't grazed since his Cambridge days: Alastair was exactly the sort of man who would have featured in one of his outlandish fantasies about abductions or ransoming. He'd abandoned them in his youth, which was where such silly things should stay.

But David did not wish to disrobe while Alastair

occupied his own head for fear of what he might accidentally think. The thought was too mortifying. Inevitably, he might also wonder what Alastair thought of his nudity, though the answer did not matter at all under the circumstances.

He was nibbling smoked cheese, apparently a favorite of Alastair's and something they'd learned he could experience again if David ate it, when Musgrave showed Paul and Lennie to the dining room.

David had not finished saying, "Thank you, Musgrave," before Lennie's quiet, but pointed, "What the fuck?"

Paul seemed to take this as some sort of cue and sat in the chair to David's right, removing his hat and placing it atop a sideboard before he did. Perhaps because there could be no privacy—David was housing his dead husband, after all—Paul did not feign ignorance or ask if he should leave the room out of politeness.

Not that either Apollyon was generally polite for the sake of politeness.

"Why?" asked Lennie. "And why the hell would you keep it from me?"

Sighing, appreciating that Alastair had gone silent within his head for the moment, David said, "Do you really think Ralph would have left you alone?"

Now that this conversation was happening, he found he was less intimidated by it.

He had not really imagined how it would go, and foolishly hoped it would never need to happen. All he had really *known* was Lennie would feel betrayed in some manner—and perhaps that their sense of rightness probably did not include killing, as such.

"He's never left me alone in my life. I've still managed."

"And when we met, you were terrified of him."

Lennie, standing at the foot of the table, rested both of their palms on the glossy mahogany and closed their mouth. They inhaled through their nose as they scowled, appearing to war with their fury rather than verbalize all of it properly.

David, though he was unrepentant, longed to hold them and show them through physical contact what he felt. What his reasoning had been. It was too hard to explain through words, which he was not adept at using under the best of circumstances. Though he was improving, he feared he was not good enough yet to explain this away. Not that he begrudged them their anger.

"Yet I've never *really* thought of killing him."

"Congratulations, then. You are a better person than me." David did not want to press the matter, and he wasn't being at all sarcastic.

He wouldn't ask if Lennie had ever thought of Ralph dying, or letting him die. It might indicate a level of desperation. David had no doubt it was Lennie's mother's influence which helped temper them into something gentler than he would ever be. He'd had no such saintly, sweet authority in his own life.

David took a breath of his own, one that mirrored Lennie's from a moment before. He presently realized an underlying truth: his bloodline boasted hunters, and he'd hunted. Yet revenge had not motivated David *entirely*, but a certain desperation to protect Lennie had.

Later, he might examine if that were enough to absolve him, as well as consider if he was a protector rather than a hunter. Benson claimed witch-hunters could be in this modern world.

But it was undeniable that vengeance had been present in David's motivation, so perhaps he shared something with his more heartless, mercurial relatives after all.

"I knew that already," Lennie said, shaking their head.

Paul transmuted what was likely a chuckle into a cough. When David glanced at him, he was reaching for a bit of the smoked cheese.

Quiet fell, punctuated only by the ticking of the grandfather clock.

"Now what?" David asked.

Lennie shook their head. "You're mostly getting out of this conversation because I didn't expect it to be a four-person affair. We *shall* have it later."

"I could remove myself," said Paul.

"You could," replied David. "I don't know how Alastair could."

I reckon you have a good point, there. I still think the only reason I can go so far from The Shuck is, well, you.

For the first time since Lennie and Paul had entered the room, David returned his attention to Alastair, following the inward pull and concentrating on his voice.

"Could I remove him, as well as me?"

It took a moment for David to realize Paul spoke, and the question was about possession. He was asking, and not with just a small amount of hope, if Alastair could use his body the way David's was being used. What was more, it almost seemed like he knew it was a possibility.

David considered it before Alastair could silently answer and distract him within his own mind. The shortest response to the question was, David did not know himself. But if one remembered all of the ghost stories, all of the folklore about specters, and even some Christian beliefs—it seemed anyone could be possessed. In fact, that was a source of great fear for the devout, if David recalled correctly.

Or, maybe one was supposed to assume all ghosts were demons? He'd never been terribly attentive to matters of theology.

"What will happen if Paul can't?" Lennie asked, rather sharply to David's ear.

Alastair answered within his head, before David could verbalize anything. *Feel like, if it doesn't work... I'll just be back in The Shuck instead of here with you three. It yanked me back when I tried to leave, myself, so... I assume it would just do the same, now.*

"And if it's anything like what happened last time," Lennie continued, "David, you're going to be fucking tired."

As was his wont, Paul was silent. But when David looked at him, his eyes were eager and soft. Those eyes, in turn, softened David. He was trying to be himself more than he paid attention to the specter he carried. Yet Alastair's own sense of eagerness matched Paul's expression. David found it hard to put aside; it permeated his mind.

"I suppose," David said, directing his words at Paul, who had put down his cheese. "If you want to try, and he wants to try—which he does—let's try."

Let go of me, David, and I'll attempt not to leave you too shattered, Alastair told him. David was willing to trust. He endeavored to actively relinquish whatever hold his being had upon Alastair's, and either the ghost or himself reached for Paul's hand.

Though Paul hesitated the slightest bit when David reached for him, Paul's fingers did clasp his own. Watching like a bird of prey, or a pickpocket ready to strike, Lennie stepped around the table and closer to David. He was glad they did, for the first time Alastair left his body, he'd collapsed. It wasn't lost on him that whatever conflict Lennie did feel toward him, they were still ready to make sure he would be all right.

He smiled, and Lennie smiled—just a little bit—back. Perhaps that relaxed him enough for the transfer to take place.

One second, Alastair was still with him, and in the next, Paul had staggered forward slightly, as though he'd tripped on a loose stone. There was that now-familiar, little spark of light, between David and Paul's hands.

David expected to faint, but he remained completely upright. Perhaps his body was growing used to the strange activities he now insisted upon undertaking. Releasing a relieved breath, he took a seat in his chair and regarded Paul, whose face had not changed physically but was, nonetheless, subtly different.

Realizing how odd it must have looked to Lennie when they'd initially seen him in the same state, David turned his head wanly and sought their eyes. They were looking rather peaceably at him given the circumstances.

It wasn't horrific, but it was eerie, to watch Paul's expressions animated with those of another person's. David would have taken Alastair back to Cromer himself without complaint. But David knew that he and Paul would relish the time together, as outlandish as it was. And like Lennie, he had no desire to conduct more private conversations while housing another soul next to his own.

Once the landlord and the smuggler were back in their home, they could separate again. David knew it as surely as he knew a coin tossed up would come back down. He couldn't explain it, but he didn't need to for it to make sense.

"Now, we have to talk." Lennie sat on the edge of the dining table that cost more than many men made in a year. They shook their head a little. As ever, David admired their lack of studied decorum. "No excuses."

Before David could respond, Paul said, "We shall see you in Cromer." He added, "Whenever... you do return." His voice was his own, quiet, bearing vowels from the place he'd never left.

Then Alastair came to the fore, saying in a way that could only belong to him, even if it was Paul's voice, "Don't fucking fall out over this, you two." It did sound much more like Portobello than Cromer.

Lennie looked as though they might like to hit Paul—or Alastair, as it were—just a little bit. But they also appeared to restrain themself. "I don't want to stay angry," they said. "I want to *understand* what was going through that Cambridge-educated head of his."

David scoffed. "He *didn't like* how a man lurking in the proverbial shadows could leap out any moment and make you feel like a pile of dog—"

"I've already said I'm not making this a four-man conversation." Lennie's voice rose by the end of their sentence. David endeavored to respect their wishes in this, even if he'd failed for the first weeks of their arrangement to comport himself with pure honesty. Lennie nodded at Paul, who rose and went for the dining room's door. "Go catch a train. You might be bloody tired when he jumps out of you, Paul. May as well get home to your own bed, though it'll be late."

Wry, finding he was less unprepared to be alone with Lennie than he'd thought, David said to Paul's slender back while he retrieved his hat from the sideboard, "Enjoy the time together."

It was a small victory when Lennie laughed a bit, low in their throat. "Those two? They absolutely will." Then, they leveled their warm bronze eyes upon David once Paul had gone, taking Alastair with him. "Why'd you lie?"

He should have known they would go immediately for the problem. He steeled himself with a breath. "It wasn't lying."

Pursing their lips, Lennie gave a noise of clear frustration. "No?"

"You never *asked* me if I was..." David lowered his voice. Everybody but Musgrave had gone home, but if he overheard any talk of murder, he might well alert the authorities. "Planning to murder your stepfather."

"You fucking oily, toffee—" Lennie halted themself, possibly due to David's look of hurt.

David could not see his own expression, naturally, but he wagered he'd winced at the words. They were so like what he'd once expected everyone thought about him, it was difficult to resist wincing. Even if, as he knew, Lennie was livid and had every right to be.

It was a good sign that Lennie did not wish to wound him properly. They *were* going straight for the heart of the matter, but seemed to rein themself in from being too savage in their insults.

In some manner, David understood their anger on the simplest of levels. When Theo had run directly to Cromer in pursuit of his skin and David had no choice but to trail behind him the morning after, the sense he'd been lied to, that something had been withheld from him, was strong and painful.

David knew now that he'd been right, or at least his instincts had been. His logic had tried to pin them to the idea that Theo had conducted an assignation with Tom. Ruefully, he reflected upon how he'd been a different person then. Worrying about an assignation was the most mundane thing he could have worried about, the sort of thing men of his ilk *would* worry about because they were not witch-hunters, or seers, or witches, or rubbed shoulders with selkies.

The circumstances that angered Lennie were different, too. David knew he needed to honor that difference, or his relationship with Lennie might be sacrificed by his own too-intense sense of rightness. Already, circumstances were so precarious in some senses, with both of them from incongruent social domains. He didn't need to muck things up with his own missteps.

It was still new and he did not want it to end; he wanted ages of loving and bickering and working and—

"Fucking beautiful, demented man," Lennie started up again. "I'd be less overset if you had just *said to me* what you wanted to do. I would have told you not to try. Ralph was dying anyway. I snuck out to see him for myself, you know. The first night we had to ourselves in Norwich, I went. I knew, then, how badly off he was."

This admission, supplied with a small note of remorse, neither bothered nor startled David. Very quietly, barely above a whisper, he said, "My father lasted for years beyond what doctors said he would. He lingered and it was... hellish. I've never spoken much about it." It had been, even though he and Theo had carved out some happiness under Father's nose. "I wouldn't have wished that on you."

To his surprise, partially because he was studying the flocked, yellow wallpaper some distance away from where he sat and deciding he did not like it, Lennie gently took his hand. "David, he was poor." They paused. "He *was* a fucker, and fuckers do tend to hang on the longest, don't they? But he never had the nutrition your father did, for one thing."

David hadn't considered it.

Lennie continued, "Sometimes, I did wonder why he wouldn't just die. Why my mum went first. I hated him. Still, I hate him. It just feels less urgent, my hate. But when I realized how ill he actually was, I didn't get the sense he'd linger for long."

"Did you have any premonitions about it?"

"No. None about Ralph's death. Funny, that." Lennie squeezed his hand and said grudgingly, after they seemed to gather their thoughts, "It's not the killing part. I like your ruthlessness, if I'm being honest. And make no mistake, he wasn't a joy unto others. But keeping me out of this, it feels a little like the schemes he had, the..." their slightly hoarse voice fell quiet. Then, they concluded with, "You lied by exclusion."

"I won't do it again, by omission or otherwise. Unless... surprises, maybe. Christmas gifts. Birthday gifts."

"I should ban you from surprising me for life," said Lennie.

Contrite, David said, "If a lifetime ban is what you see fit to do, I'll accept it."

But Lennie shook their head, removing their cap, a newer and cleaner version in the flat style they favored, and said after a moment, "I can't believe he's gone. I almost fainted outside the house, if you can imagine me fainting."

"Wait, you went..." David stroked their palm with

his thumb. "You saw Robbie before you came here. You must have."

"Paul had a premonition."

Having it confirmed that Paul was no longer stopping himself from seeing the future did lighten David's heart somewhat. He hoped Benson knew, too, as the old man was deeply attached to Paul, in spite of all his gruff bluster. "Well, that's something."

"From it, we sort of surmised where you'd gone. Then I found that note."

David glanced at them and couldn't help but smile. "I don't imagine, if the premonition suggested what would happen, my note wasn't suspicious."

"What was your plan, then?" Lennie murmured, and as though to show their anger was cooling, they brought the back of David's hand to their lips and brushed it with a kiss. "Pretend he'd just died? That you'd just gone to Norwich for some business emergency, even though I handle so many of your affairs?"

It was lovely to be so known. David did not bristle under the gentle teasing. "Yes. More or less. And Robbie agreed with me, the fool."

Sighing, Lennie said, with an air of resignation, "I told him to come here if he couldn't be by himself. Tonight, I mean. I assume we could just be back in Cromer tomorrow, seeing as you do like it better."

Of course Lennie had suggested it. They were kinder than David could ever be.

"Then I'd best hold off on seducing you by way of apology. Just in case he pays us a visit."

18

Cromer

The taproom wobbled a bit, its old wood floor wriggling because he was slightly intoxicated. Tom belatedly remembered that the unpleasant sensation of wriggling floors was one of the many reasons he'd been so glad to give up drink. There was a list from here to the moon, most days. Regardless, he was only human, and he was rather drunk for the first time in months.

Now, the list of reasons seemed as far away as the moon, rather than capable of reaching it when compiled. It had been an impeccable idea when, as he considered the enormous ramifications of possibly imminent murder and all the undercurrents of love in his life, to drink.

Benson was no help, for he'd never practiced moderation and said they may as well have something to take the edge off wondering whether David would next return to The Shuck a murderer.

As Paul entered the taproom for the first time at nine when he had already said he would be out, Tom could not help but call to him, "You're late." He also noted how the colors around Paul were no longer just deep greens, but a watercolor-like swirl of greens and burnished rust. It was exquisite, if unexpected.

It didn't matter much if Paul was here. Folks had dwindled, as they were sometimes liable to do this time of the evening. Work was to be had in the morning, and for the most part, The Shuck's clientele were respectable enough these days to have schedules that demanded their attention rather early.

He did not expect his uncle to smile almost roguishly and say, sounding more like the ill-tempered Mr. James Gow than himself, "Can't be late in my own establishment."

Tom set aside the small bottle of brandy he'd been clandestinely nursing. He'd had enough if he was hearing accents wrong. But Benson, who'd been lingering near the bar all afternoon and into the evening, as though to mind Tom while Theo was at home and Paul was accompanying Lennie, said, "Lad, it's not you. Neither you nor your brandy."

"What do you mean?"

Nodding to Paul, who was cheerfully coming their way, Benson murmured, "They're mad."

"They?" Unlike Lennie, Paul had never been addressed as such. Not to Tom's knowledge.

"Your uncle," said Benson. He sighed. "And your other uncle, if I'm being truthful. That's what Alastair was, wasn't he?"

Deliberating, Tom wasn't sure. He and Alastair never had even the taciturn, fraught familial relationship he and Paul had possessed for the first part of his life. But if Benson referred to Paul and Alastair's essentially married state, then Tom conceded he could well have had another uncle by marriage.

More to the point, he still didn't quite understand what Benson meant.

"I don't see what all your fuss is about, Benson," said Paul. This time, it was his usual voice. It seemed to Tom that Benson was having trouble looking at Paul, as though he either glowed brightly like the sun, or had somehow caused a vulgar offense that led everyone else to glance away in slight discomfort. "This is fine."

"It's not natural," said Benson. He swilled his pint. "It's not the right order of things." He took another sip.

"Are any of *us* given to that?" Paul asked. Tom took it to mean any of them. In that regard, Paul asked a good question. Though things had grown tiresomely complicated of late, Tom marveled at how much had shifted within the last year or thereabouts, how he no longer felt so singular as to drive himself to extreme actions.

"Don't be difficult," said Benson. "Whenever I said you should let yourself dream again—and open up to anything that brought—I didn't mean *let a ghost inhabit your body*."

"Oh," said Tom. "My god." That would certainly account for Portobello coming through where there should've been various shades of a Norfolk drawl. He stared at Paul anew. "I didn't know *you* could do that."

Benson sounded purely disdainful. "Anyone can. They'll pounce on anybody." In that case, Tom took *they'll* to mean ghosts. "It's the seeing and the hearing and the talking to them that most folks can't do." Pointedly, he added, fixing Paul with a muzzy look, "But this isn't right. You know that, Paul."

"Him being dead isn't the right order of things," Paul retorted.

"So you'll cart him around until the end of your days?"

"I already was. This is just more expedient." But Paul softened slightly, and added, "I won't do it forever."

With a blink, Tom silently admitted that was true: Paul *had* been carrying Alastair in memory.

"No," said Benson. "You were carrying grief, not him. It's different. And you shouldn't keep him here... even if you want to host him in your dreams every night."

Glancing from Benson's grave, craggy face to Paul's more intransigent one, Tom ventured to say, "David slept for days, after he..." He meant only to suggest Paul might suffer similarly, having gone from no contact with the dead at all to possibly too much in one go. He did not judge his uncle for having done this the way Benson clearly did. Tom felt, and it did seem he and Paul were made of similar stuff, he would make the same choice if Theo were a ghost.

At present, he felt distant from Theo, but that didn't change the love he had for him.

Tom could tell Theo wondered what he'd said wrong. Tom still did not have the courage to tell him that wasn't the trouble. He didn't possess the fortitude to speak about anything he thought, for fear Theo would see the merits of his fears. Or their inevitability. And leave.

Ever since Theo changed on the beach in front of him, it felt like they were separated by a wealth of per-spective and experience Tom would never have, could never have. Beyond that, he still couldn't shake the thought he might be keeping Theo from feeling the best he could. If Theo had healed so readily when a seal, he should spend more time in the water as a crea-ture who was completely unintelligible to Tom.

Yet he would not, so long as Tom remained.

Perhaps at the heart of the selkie myths, the skin was not the largest source of conflict so much as two utterly separate sets of needs and desires. The best Tom could say for himself was he'd relinquished con-trol when he'd given Theo back his skin.

He could not abandon the idea that Theo was meant for a more expansive or unfettered existence than the one they'd created since last winter. Even when Tom had wandered, drifted, gone from trade to trade so long as it was near water, he was never a wild creature of old lore. Theo, however, was. One morn-ing, he might wake and realize he'd wasted his time, deciding such narrow domesticity was wearisome.

"I don't mind being *a bit tired* when all of this is through," said Paul. "What's exhaustion to me?"

With the air of a schoolmarm who was trying to explain the simplest of equations to a bright student behaving errantly, Benson said, "This can't be why he's lingering. It can't have been because he wants this."

"He's *right* here, you know." It was Alastair rather than Paul speaking that time. Tom chuckled.

"You're naughty, aren't you?" Benson said. "Should have stuck to illegal activities in his dreams."

"Benson, calm down," said Alastair-through-Paul. "We only did this because Lennie wanted to talk to David privately."

It didn't assuage Benson, who, like most men who were told to calm down, did not. "Doesn't make it right."

"Did David kill him?"

"Pardon?" Alastair-through-Paul glanced at Tom. It was unnerving; Paul still looked as he always did.

Same coloring, same tousled hair under his old hat. But his minute expressions weren't entirely his own.

"That *was* why he went to Norwich all of a sudden, was it not?"

"He didn't do a thing to Lennie's stepfather."

"Shame."

Now Alastair-through-Paul seemed to infer he was drunk in that instant, for he asked with a shade of amusement, "Been drinking?"

"What about me wanting a terrible old man to be dead suggests I've been drinking?"

It was the thing that got through to Paul, however. The next answer Tom received was all his uncle. "Tom, go home."

He frowned. Home was the last place he wished to go.

~

ORDINARILY, Theo tried to take his leisure with Tom so their time off would coincide. But he needed some hours to himself to think, so he'd elected to remain in the cottage while Tom was at The Shuck this evening.

When the clock struck five, he fretted that Tom might be avoiding him. Paul was scheduled to take Tom's place, so far as he knew.

Six came, then seven, then eight. Nine, then a little after. Theo made himself something to eat, not feeling particularly hungry, but recognizing he'd be less able to converse without food in his stomach. Tom had to come home, sometime, and he wasn't the sort to stay out all night. Theo supposed he always had the option of staying in The Shuck if he wished, but hoped he would return.

They hadn't fought. They hadn't even bickered.

Best he could tell, the flow of warmth and understanding between them had changed and slowed sometime close to when he'd shifted on the beach. It had certainly soured when he'd tried to explain why disclosing David and Alastair's plan to Lennie might not be the best option.

Navigating these more vulnerable circumstances was disconcertingly new. He'd never told a partner about his preternatural state while he was still within the relationship.

There was a link between his identity and Tom's newfound hesitation; he just didn't know what the link signified. He was not at all nervous he might be held against his will. Tom's change in demeanor seemed more to do with himself. Theo would wager it was something Tom had experienced inwardly and just wasn't expressing. That *did* worry him a little. When they'd met, Tom had been so guarded.

It was no one's responsibility but Tom's to let down that guardedness, yet Theo did wish he would remember he was well loved and safe to do so. Because he *was* loved, from all quarters.

However, Theo had a hunch he knew what was in Tom's heart, as well as how he might help remedy it. Or, at least, to demonstrate he was serious and willing to help move forward. He sighed and squirmed a little in the armchair, casting a sad eye to the remnants of buttered bread and cheddar on the plate before him. He'd left the stoneware plate on an end table next to the chair, caring not at all to eat at the proper table.

His lover returned when it was about half-past nine, which was good for Theo's nerves. He hadn't considered what he would do if it grew much later. Usually, he could be quite patient, but once he'd made up his mind about this, it was difficult to be serene.

He stood immediately as Tom entered the room, not that there was an excess of space for either of them to navigate inside their home. "May we talk?"

There was no mistaking the relief on Tom's face. He said, "Thank Christ you asked first."

"There's no shame in asking," said Theo, softening it even further with a small smile.

"No, none," said Tom, "but I didn't know how." He stood there, all of his indecision and nerves written upon his mien for Theo to read.

Troubled, but not overly, Theo went to him. "You smell of brandy."

Tom's mouth opened, then closed. He looked at Theo with some embarrassment. Without hesitation, Theo took both of his hands, looking at him from the narrow distance that spanned their bodies.

"I know. I got nervous," Tom said. "If you want to wait to talk until tomorrow, I shall understand." It was a point of pride, Theo knew, in all the stops and starts Tom had while giving up the majority of alcohol, that they'd never had an important discussion if he was too intoxicated to be sensible. In this second, though, Theo didn't believe him to be incapacitated. He just seemed, as he'd said, nervous.

"I don't think my heart could take waiting," Theo said, "and you aren't *so* drunk. I don't even think you're drunk."

Sighing, he said, "No, I didn't even have *that* much brandy. My tolerance has gone down. Regardless, the walk here did me good." He rested his forehead gently against Theo's. "I just didn't want you to think I was trying to make you feel sorry for me. Not at all."

"I never do." Theo smiled, luxuriating in the wafts of Jicky drifting from Tom's jumper. He could only catch them when Tom was close, possibly because his nose had grown used to the perfume.

"Good. You shouldn't."

Before Theo could lose his resolve, he did something abrupt. "I want you to have it." He felt the frown in Tom's forehead rather than saw it. Fair enough; it was a complete non sequitur and Tom could not have noticed the soft pelt in the wingback, still warm from where Theo had been half-sitting on it.

"I already told you last week; I don't think the mallard jacket will suit me. If you must give it away, try Paul. I'm a little paler than him. I was thinking he could wear that shade of green."

"No," said Theo, and he had to chuckle at the jacket's mention, "not that—I decided to keep it for myself."

"What, then?"

Drawing away from him enough to look him in the eyes, Theo found it was more difficult to speak than to show him. What he'd decided to do went against everything his father had cautioned him against, but he felt no fear. He relinquished one of Tom's hands and led him to the wingback.

Without a word, he picked up the skin and gently pressed it into Tom's grasp.

Staring at it in the warm candlelight, Tom was silent.

"Feels wonderful when *you* hold it." Really, it should sound salacious; it didn't.

Although, if Theo were to be blunt, part of the sensation that permeated him was erotic. He wondered, very briefly, if his father had ever experienced something of the kind. As quickly as the thought arrived, he dismissed it. He didn't want to waste time thinking about what would only sadden him. Given all he knew about Father and certainly his mother, he thought the answer would be no.

"I haven't even... you haven't..." Apparently stunned by the offering, Tom muttered, "We haven't even talked."

"I know," said Theo, "and we will talk. This isn't in lieu of talking. I just felt like I needed to do it. Now."

At that, Tom's eyes were on Theo's, not Theo's skin. "Mr. Harper, you'd do something like this on an impulse?"

"Even someone old and set in their habits might have an impulse. Look at Benson," said Theo. He shivered when Tom's pointer finger idly petted his skin. It undeniably resulted in a gratifying sensation. "This is the best one I've had in an age, I think. Apart from the impulse that saw me dragging a petulant Mr. Drunkard from inky water so he wouldn't be pulled out to Shipden to become another ghost."

Despite the warmth and levity of their present tenor, something about his words seemed to cause Tom some thought.

Theo waited. When Tom clearly tried to begin a sentence, then swallowed down what he was about to say, Theo guided him to the sofa near the window. Gently, he pushed him to sit. Tom sat, holding Theo's skin as though it were some precious, irreplaceable curio.

Then Theo directed him as compassionately as he could to bare his thoughts. "Tell me."

"I'm not extraordinary enough for you."

"What do you mean?"

"You can hear things a mile away, and you can heal yourself if you just go out into the sea..."

"If I change in the sea."

"Yes." Tom looked up at him. "But it's even more

than that, I fear. You're older than I'll ever be, and you've seen things I've only read about in books. I'll never have the outlook that you do, or the wisdom, or the patience." Seeming pained, he said, "My father died young; it was something about his heart." His right thumb moved restlessly on Theo's skin, and in turn, it made Theo restless. It was a far different touch from that of a moment ago. "Like Alastair, too, I suppose. I don't know if the same will happen to me—Paul is older than Father was, and he seems fine, but I've also abused myself with drink, so who knows?"

"Darling," Theo began, the yearning to comfort Tom so acute that it almost hurt his chest. "I love how you see me, but I'm..." He shook his head and sat closely next to Tom. "I'm a man, not some demigod." Releasing a breath as he realized this had been bubbling under their daily routines, he said, "I don't see myself as better than you. I'm not just waiting until you die, and you're not forcing me to be here with you."

So quietly, Tom asked, "Am I worth it?"

Stunned by the question, Theo leaned over and kissed him briefly on the cheek. "Yes."

"It'll hurt when I die, and you'll have given up so much to be with me."

Better than most would, Theo knew why Tom would be thinking about it. Paul, or Paul as he had once been, was an icon of love and loss. With a small note of humor, Theo said, "The first bit—everyone dies, and if you're lucky enough to be loved, death hurts anybody left behind." He didn't think too much about whether Tom might die early, even though it had clearly been on Tom's mind.

"What about the second bit?"

Theo kissed him again in the same place. "Well..."

He thought of what to say. He didn't hate being a seal, and it did give him a measure of excess energy, restlessness, really, to be near the sea while human. The ocean did beckon him. He wouldn't deny it. "Every day I'm here, I'm also giving up *very* cold water, and lots of darkness, and endless amounts of fish. Did you ever think that perhaps I like *you* much more than those things? Being a selkie isn't all better healing and a longer life. I'll have you know, too, that I can be felled by an accident or a serious illness."

Tom chuckled. "At least *I'm* not beholden to a bit of fur." He petted it once more, and this time, it felt immeasurably good.

"Stop that," said Theo, although he was sure it sounded more like, *Keep going.*

"Ah," said Tom, watching Theo closely, "seems like this thing isn't just used to control you. Or it doesn't have to be. It could be used for other endeavors."

"We'll have to experiment to find the answer," said Theo. When Tom tilted his head for a kiss on the lips rather than the cheek, he was ready to oblige.

19

———

Norwich

The discussion ended, like so many of theirs had so far, in David's bed. He hadn't *meant* to seduce Lennie. But Lennie seemed tacitly hellbent on being seduced, and so, it happened.

If David were thinking clearly—which he wasn't at all—he might realize the seduction boded well. It wasn't a final goodbye or a sendoff; it was the sort of seduction that heralded a new direction. One in which he'd not go around contemplating and enacting murder plans without Lennie's express consent. Had there been any ability left for him to think clearly, he would also have realized that he had not seduced Lennie. They had seduced him, which must indicate good things for the state of their arrangement.

Of all the things that David surmised were in their future together, many of which likely involved a taciturn witch and his equally taciturn uncle who happened to be a seer, as well as the taciturn witch's selkie companion, murder was not something he'd anticipate again.

Presently curled on their side, Lennie said, "Did

you and Benson ever learn how you knocked out Robbie?"

David was far from thinking about that night, and he had to take a few moments to realize what Lennie meant. He skimmed his fingers along their shoulder. "Oh, that... no, not Benson. Alastair. Well, in passing. Alastair helped me understand it."

"Suppose a man terrified of ghosts wouldn't be able to tell you much more than he did already," Lennie said affably.

"When Alastair and I first tried to channel, and he was..." David paused, for there was no way to say it that didn't sound vulgar. "In me..."

"Sounds unfit for polite company."

"I'm not telling polite company; I'm telling you."

Lennie chuckled. "True. Go on, then."

"It felt the same as when the spark left me and hit Robbie's massive chest. Like static, almost." Pensively, he said, "I saw it when I let Alastair go to Paul."

"I'm certain that if you tell Benson, he'll come up with some longwinded explanation about souls and energies and witch-hunters and necromancy that we can only half-follow."

Kissing the side of their throat he could reach, David agreed. "It does seem witch-hunter is a wider term than I first thought." Then he thought of a question for Lennie. "Why do you think Paul's vision was wrong?"

Earlier, they'd both briefly covered the contents. Rather, Lennie had communicated the contents.

This left David to ponder if it was the first premonition Paul Apollyon had seen that wasn't true, or if he was merely out of practice. But shortly after being told anything about the sight of Alastair looming over Ralph like an omen of death, David found he wanted to concentrate much more on what Lennie wished to do to his prick.

He'd let the matter go.

Now, at half-past two in the morning and with his ardor seen to, he felt more equipped to ask sensibly.

"I don't think it was."

"Well, it... yes, it was. Ralph didn't die by Alastair's hand, or mine."

Tolerantly, Lennie murmured, "Sometimes, premonitions can show us possibilities. That doesn't happen much to me. They also... they can come across garbled, or... metaphor-like. I know my premonitions can occasionally feel the same as one of those fables with all the animals. They make sense, but they're strange."

"Aesop's?"

"Yes. It might not signify anything immediately. Then, you step back and think about matters. Everything you've seen actually means something else."

Rather charmed and amused, David said, "So, symbolically, Paul might have seen Alastair because *I* was carrying Alastair."

"Yes, exactly. He saw truth, but not the way most people would."

"Did your mother see possibilities?" He was genuinely intrigued. He knew Lennie loved their mother, and she had taught them most about magic and things otherworldly.

"She only mentioned it a few times," said Lennie. "But she saw things that could have happened. The way she explained it... she'd see almost the same vision more than once, only specific things within it would change. Best as she could figure, they were probably different outcomes for a situation. Not that anybody can properly compare them to know."

"Sounds..." David sighed. "Terrifying, in fact."

"If you're not used to it, I imagine it would be. And it didn't seem to happen nearly as much as her ordinary premonitions."

Heaven help him. He was at a point in his life when the phrase *ordinary premonitions* resonated and actually meant something realistic. "Then, maybe—" David swallowed the very words. Now that he had not succeeded in killing Ralph, he didn't truly want to contemplate a world where he had.

"If Paul saw an aftermath, say... it could have happened. If the wind had blown harder on a leaf that morning, or a bee had landed on a different flower. I think, at least, that's how it works." They must have sensed David's disquiet, for they rolled over and faced him, meeting his eyes with intensity.

He reached for them, and they came closer, nestling against his chest. "Just to be clear, I am glad I didn't succeed."

To his surprise, Lennie laughed quietly. "I wonder what you would have done in your own head while Alastair did the deed. You can hardly stand and face a corner with your fingers in your ears in your own mind, can you?"

"God," said David. "You've attached yourself to a rather idiotic man, I think. You should ask Theo and Tom if they want a third and spare yourself the trouble of being so intimately near me."

Lennie beamed. "They would take us as a pair, or not at all. But you may have a good idea—between the three of us, we could keep you right."

"Am I so bad?"

Playfully, Lennie said, "On my own, I've quite a challenge ahead of me. Especially if I bring out your protective instincts." They kissed the edge of his collarbone.

He could not deny they did: when there came a shuffle from downstairs, Lennie might have been first out of bed. But David was first out of the room bearing a large, antique brass candelabra. Even though they jostled him to get out of the way, he still burst through the open doorway before they could.

"I had so hoped for a night to ourselves, you know," he said, just over his shoulder. In the best of cases, Robbie might've caused the noise, which was still not a good case in David's estimation.

"It could be nothing at all." Lennie mirrored his quiet speaking.

"If you'd said that to me several months ago, I might be inclined to agree. But now? Who knows."

~

HE WAS OBVIOUSLY unwilling to allow Lennie to face any potential threat first. While they might not have admitted it because it did not fit with their image and they were perfectly able to take care of themself, they rather liked being so protected.

When they silently acknowledged the feeling, they were happier to let David precede them downstairs. Regardless of how it warmed them through, Lennie was still not best pleased to rise.

They were *direly* displeased to see that the source of the soft sounds—really, had David not seemed so out of sorts after the day's events, Lennie would have ignored them—was Robbie.

"I told him not to break in," they whispered. Of course, he had.

"How long has he been down here?" David seemed more bemused than angry.

He struck a match and lit the three candlesticks in the candelabra, although they both could make Robbie out in the bright moonlight that pervaded the room.

Snorting, Lennie shrugged. Robbie was presently strewn on a rug. Perhaps him falling from the sofa to the floor had been the source of the shuffling. Maybe the final, muffled thump of his body hitting the floor was the noise that really reached upstairs. Lennie couldn't say.

But they did answer David. "I couldn't tell you. He sleeps like the dead, if that's not too soon to say. Falling like that wouldn't have woken him. I think we'd best leave him on the floor." They looked around the ground-floor parlor.

"I'm not leaving a man on the carpet in my own home. There are bedrooms upstairs."

"Not even Robbie?"

"No. He'd terrify Mrs. Greaves, for one thing. Or Ellie. Or Musgrave. Anybody who works here and might come across him."

David nudged Robbie's shoulder with the tip of his big toe, then did so with a little more force. Lennie almost reminded him he was naked, and they were naked. Robbie and Lennie had grown up with casual nudity, having lived in such close quarters, so Robbie likely wouldn't mind. The neighbors, too, were not always given to decency. Overall, the Campling children retained a sense of worldliness concerning the body from an early age.

From what Lennie was given to understand, the Mills household had not been nearly so prosaic.

Robbie woke without a start, presumably because

he was just that tired. He sat up, first focusing on David's feet, then his calves, then his thighs.

"I'll grant you, you don't look like some coddled scholar-type." Then his eyes found Lennie, and he said, "I wasn't gonna break in, then it got late. They took *him* late, I ate late because Mrs. Wills insisted I eat one of her pies, and then I sat there for a bit before I decided I couldn't take it. You were abed. House was dark. That butler or whoever he is... he must've gone to sleep. Or home. I knocked and no one answered."

Sighing, Lennie extended a hand and helped haul him up. He was larger than them, but they were strong. "It might be better we found you now. You'd have given us a fright come morning."

They did not want to elaborate upon why neither they nor David had heard Robbie knocking.

Nudity was one thing; recounting sexual exploits to their stepbrother was quite another. Besides, he'd already heard at least some of what had transpired, if he'd been inside long enough to fall asleep on a sofa.

"You'd have given *Musgrave* a fright in the morning," said David. "Or very likely Mrs. Greaves, depending on who entered the parlor first." He turned his back on Robbie but still spoke to him. "Come along. You can use a bedroom."

Evidently, Robbie had been expecting to be turned out. He gawped at Lennie, who shrugged and nodded toward David's back. Robbie followed David, and Lennie followed Robbie.

"Why *did* you come to Cromer to see me, before?" asked David, his back still turned.

"I..." Robbie blushed, if not mortified by David's nakedness, then embarrassed by what he was about to say. "I was losing my nerve. Wanted to tell you so."

"Ah, I'd wondered if that might be it. Don't dawdle,

man. I don't want to find I'm missing my mother's porcelain figurines of dogs, come morning."

"You'd best do as he says," Lennie said. They eyed one of the said figurines as they passed it on a little table in the hallway. The tiny white and blue dogs were ugly, but reputedly quite valuable, and they glinted in the diffuse moonlight.

"What sort of a toff is he?" muttered Robbie.

"The sort who invites you to dinner or gives you a bed if you break into his house," murmured Lennie. At that, Robbie frowned at them quizzically over his shoulder, and they grinned. "No, you're right. Not you, the first time you did. But to be fair, you *were* threatening me."

"I have hope, though," David said, as he strutted through his foyer without a stitch of any of the clothing he so loved, "we can all learn to get on well, going forward."

Despite the mundane little conflicts and questions that were bound to ensue, Lennie shared the same hope. When they stopped to think about it, they actually felt it was less a hope and more an inevitability. After all, Ralph was no longer about to seep poison into the people he should have been more interested in protecting.

This was to be the first night of many more nights with Mr. Mills. Lennie knew—without needing to see it beforehand—that something very good would come of them.

Although they felt that goodness would flow from their and David's time together, once Robbie had been settled in a disused bedroom, hesitant doubt crept in.

After everything, Lennie found the quiet and lack of something to do rather unsettling. There was a little too much space to muse when they did not have a problem to solve. Something concrete, like their step-brother needing a place to sleep.

They trusted David, and despite the day's events, always would.

Still, when they were both back in his bed and David's arm was around them, they ventured, "Will we make it, do you think?"

They meant whatever tender, new relationship was still forming between them.

While their symbiosis was strong, it couldn't be denied that they each had far different upbringings and standings in life. If David didn't consider the differences an issue, which he didn't, Lennie wasn't carefree enough to believe others wouldn't.

They ached to know there wouldn't come a time when others' doubts and judgements might influence David for ill.

If they were still and listened to themself, they felt it would never arrive. That didn't mean there would never be people who judged even the business association, never mind if they understood anything beyond it. But Lennie was confident David wouldn't forsake them for the sake of appearances.

Yet they'd had to ask.

"Will we make it?" David repeated. "Sorry, I don't understand." He was tired; it showed in the sibilance of his voice. Lennie reached for his hand and squeezed it briefly.

"I feel like we're embarking on the beginning of whatever comes next," they said. "Whatever we're to be."

"You might want to ask me again in the morning," said David, as his lips brushed the side of Lennie's head in either a kiss, or just the course of his speaking. "When I'm not so slow. But I'm not giving you up so easily when I've only just found you." He could probably intuit the source of Lennie's anxiety, because he added, "And I'm not planning on dragging you to odious dinners where somebody will snidely ask which college was yours because they can *hear* you didn't go..." he yawned. "David Mills is running away from that. He's got enough money and it only stands to grow."

Lennie would not ask again in the morning, because this answer so delighted them. "It'll still be difficult."

"Us? We're not difficult." This time, David squeezed their hand.

"We're... both stubborn. But no, not us," said Lennie. "The shit around us."

David rolled properly to his side, and with his free hand, carefully and gently tilted Lennie's face to look at him in the dark. Lennie could easily see his serene expression. "Then we'll be the eye of the storm, as it were. Let the world rage as it wants. And I'll not throw you over because anybody is offended."

20

Cromer

Grief was heavier to carry than a ghost. Paul knew this, now, and he was afraid to let go of the ghost to once again take up the grief.

He had promised Benson last night that he'd let Alastair fly free, or fly back into The Shuck. But last night had turned into early morning.

He sat on the low sofa that had been in his flat since his mother and father's days of owning the pub, one which, one memorable morning, he'd come out to see Alastair sprawled on his back in a dead sleep. That was the first night of many nights Alastair was to spend in this building.

Back then, Paul had let him sleep because the whole flat smelled of spirits; it had been obvious how worn out Alastair would be when he finally did wake. But beyond kindness or pragmatism, Paul fretted that, as soon as Alastair woke up and realized he'd let himself into Paul's flat in a drunken stupor, he would leave due to the mortification.

So Paul removed his boots and covered him with a

blanket, praying to the god he didn't quite believe in that Alastair wouldn't wake up. He didn't, not until hours later, bemused and embarrassed, with the soft syllables of sleep and too much drink in his voice.

As he thought about those past moments, he didn't have to explain what he was thinking. He just said, "I hardly knew you, then. But I knew you were for me."

I knew it, too, even if I couldn't quite admit it.

They'd been talking this way for hours, now. Paul did not mind it, though his throat was sore. He waited to feel fatigued, nervous, anything negative and indicative of a specter overstaying his welcome, but none of those sensations came. He was at peace, really, the serenity in his mind mirroring what so many others seemed to see in his mien. Paul rarely felt it himself, but others often saw it.

The mode of conversing *was* somewhat odd.

Alastair could access all of what Paul thought, if his quick responses to half-formed sentences were anything to judge by, yet Paul only heard his voice. It seemed the openness only went one way, and perhaps once he was just himself again, he would research why that was. If he still cared to know when Alastair was gone.

For gone he would be—even if he was simply out of Paul's body and fixed upon The Shuck forevermore, Paul assumed he wouldn't be able to access Alastair unless it was within dreams. After all, *this* was easy, according to Benson. If Paul had known how easy, he would have offered himself up for possession immediately. He had little care for the church, next to none.

If placing his soul next to Alastair's meant damnation because it offended a deity who wished the living and dead to remain separate, it was a price he'd happily pay.

"I suppose Benson might be right. I might need to... untie you." He didn't know what else to call it.

He knew the Catholics in particular would have a bevy of words having to do with possession, but all he could think about was how it let him talk to Alastair. He had little notion of whether he'd tied their souls together, or if he was gripping a soul with his hands tightly and ignoring how it burned.

This could be like a man lost in intoxicants. Only after they wore off would certain consequences become apparent.

Ruefully, Paul released a sigh. He knew carrying on this way wasn't feasible, no matter how much he tried to rationalize it. When he was younger, he'd had visions while awake, had to live and act as though nothing was amiss while his mind's eye showed him whatever the universe had distilled for his viewing.

He could exist with part of himself inward, the other directed outward.

But he suspected that what he did right now would push that limit.

"I confess, I'm terrified that if I let you go, I'll never hear you again, or see you again, or—"

Angel, hush. I'll be right here.

"How do you know?"

Stop trying to make it make sense, came the fond reply.

Paul had to laugh at himself. Had he not said a similar thing to David, not so long ago?

"Even if you are here—and what if you get sucked back into, I don't know, the ether—I won't know. I won't know either way."

But you can dream of me. I can visit you there.

Quietly, Paul said, "Why were you still here, anyway? You weren't a bad man. I shouldn't think you'd be hell-bound, or..."

An estranged son might be a reason. Fleeing James, though understandable under the circumstances, and because Paul was so deeply in love with Alastair, was not an ideal act. Paul could both despise the son himself and admit this truth.

You. The only thing that really drove me from this building was David. As soon as that cleared up, I was back.

Paul considered it. "Just... me."

Sorry, but we seem to be bound. Handfasted, even. Paul could picture the grin on Alastair's face. The grin would probably mellow a little as Alastair added, *I'm here to look after you, I think.*

"No... there has to be a deeper reason why you're here. Again."

I thought, for a wee while, that it might be using David to commit a murder. But Ralph did nothing to you, so I can't think that was it.

Maybe, Paul mused, he *was* just here now. Imprinted or confined. "Whatever the *why* is, Benson says I shouldn't keep you..." Paul disliked the thought of *trapping* him in The Shuck.

He didn't even need to vocalize it for Alastair to respond. *Fuck Benson. Paul Apollyon, I've never been trapped in my life.*

"You're not alive." Chuckling, for he couldn't resist laughing a little at Alastair's tone, he added, "You know, if you hadn't been haunting the place, I wouldn't have opened myself back up to premonitions."

While he said it, he felt he was saying what Alastair was meant to do. What Alastair had left unfinished in his life was clear. He'd gone to bed in love and part of a community, but departed without saying a farewell. Paul was wizened enough to understand many men did not get to say goodbye, so in this, Alastair was not extraordinary.

But as a consequence of the death, Paul had denied part of himself which came naturally as breathing. He would never *blame* Alastair for that: it was his own choice. It had even made him feel better for a short time.

You always were more clever than me. It feels correct, I reckon, that I was meant to push you back into your sight.

"I have never thought you were less clever. If you can go somewhere better, please don't fucking linger around and skulk in the shadows on my account."

Nowhere better. How long was it before you decided you couldn't bear your abilities without me here?

"Not so long after James came down and took you," said Paul quietly. "I was angry that I'd seen *nothing* to do with any of it. Around the same time I started to write the letters." Absentmindedly, he promised himself he'd put them into a keepsake book, perhaps, so that he could access them properly. Not leave them in heaps.

I wish he'd not put you through it. I also wish I hadn't just... run from him as soon as he might be able to cope. But I don't wish I'd stayed with him, either. If I hadn't run... well, I believe I'd still have met you. Just... it might have taken longer.

Smiling wanly, Paul said, "I'm glad you feel so." He laid down, looking up at the ceiling, studying the crossbeams.

They each fell noiseless, Paul relishing the knowledge that he was not alone. Dreading how the moment approached when he would have to be alone, again.

I'll make a deal with you, if you want. If you stop worrying and untie me, or whatever you want to call it, I'll come to you every night until it annoys you.

"Annoy me all you like."

Alastair hardly waited for him to finish saying *like* before he said, *I'll go when you go. Odds are, you'll die in this bloody place, which would make keeping that promise easier.*

"I might not." But Paul agreed. He probably would, and it didn't trouble him.

Even if you don't, when you do, I'll find you. Hold your hand. We'll walk on together.

Firstly, Paul tried to keep back his tears, sniffling discreetly as best he could. Then, he couldn't stop the crying. But it was more of a balm than the result of frustration or bitterness.

Just trust me.

Paul let go.

He could handle being haunted in his sleep until the end of his days. Everyone else would just have to deal with a ghost in the pub for a little while longer.

IT WAS RATHER TOO early to be at The Shuck. Being there when the light was so fresh brought to mind Tom's earliest days working there, the ones when he was no longer a child but still had years of experience to gain before he could feel at all grown.

Tom smiled at Theo, who accompanied him inside. *That* part of being here was different. This morning reminded him a little of the one when he and Theo had trundled in after Theo had napped in David's empty house, only he assumed David would not be rushing to Cromer from Norwich all because of a note.

Actually, after Paul and Lennie departed for Norwich, he had not heard from either Lennie or David, and all Paul had told him was to *go home*. It seemed prudent to come in early, today of all days, partially because Tom had little idea of what was going on. Paul was here and so was Alastair—in some capacity. Lennie was presumably still in Norwich with David. Tom was almost afraid to ask how everything had actually transpired, even if he knew nobody was dead by David's hand.

However, it was also difficult to care when he remembered the way Lennie had spoken about their stepfather's revolting beliefs and habits in this very taproom. He would never have told the police if indeed David had done something. Nor would Paul, and nor would Theo, whose concern had all along been with Lennie and their potential feelings of betrayal.

He sighed and settled in one of the chairs near the great hearth. They were almost always occupied and he rarely got to sit in them. Mismatched, they still offset the space well, one red houndstooth and the other a glaringly contrasting paisley with shades of chartreuse. Theo had taken the red; he took the alarmingly bright green.

He was not really the worse for wear after slipping back into an old habit, for Theo had made him drink water and tea and monitored how much he'd consumed of both. There were advantages to one's beloved being much older, and the son of a rather arcane apothecary.

After a long night of talking, sipping tea, and bringing each other pleasure when words had fallen repetitive, they'd decided to walk out and into the morning's clouds. Sleep wasn't to be had, so it seemed better to remain awake.

For a second time, Tom had given Theo's skin back, somehow ensuring Theo was even more deeply smitten. He did say he would act as its custodian, take care of it, and make sure it never came to harm, but he reiterated his intent had never been to capture. The skin was, and always would be, Theo's own to take as he wished.

Even to take wherever else he wished, if things ever changed to that degree.

After a leisurely walk from the cottage to the promenade, The Shuck seemed the correct destination.

"You know, if you ever feel like I say something outlandish and callous again, just tell me right that instant. You might be correct. I *am* older than you. I'm older than Benson." Theo studied Tom's expression, outwardly intent upon making the point. "I know it lends me a different perspective."

It certainly did, one that would remain alien to Tom. He believed that would need to become one of the many things he thought was beautiful about Theo. In a sense, he already thought it was, even if it jostled his sense of self. Sometimes, the best, most vital things did.

"Well," said Tom. "You've just lived long enough to see more of the cycles the rest of us take for granted. And it wasn't just what you said about shielding Lennie." He let his head loll back a bit against the worn, comfortable cushions of the green chair. "When I realized your burn was healed when you were a seal, I..."

"What?"

"I worried. I worried I kept you from a healthier,

perhaps better, life. I didn't feel I was as bad as those men who steal selkies' skins, but I wondered if I was somehow keeping you from... I don't know, being who you were."

If this caused Theo any sorrow, Tom didn't see it. He sighed, eyeing Tom with such a deep affection it could have filled the room of its own accord, and shook his head. There was an instant when Theo felt exactly like the stranger who'd rescued him from drowning, and indeed from becoming a ghost in the depths. The same attraction, the same warmth, spread from Theo to Tom in ripples.

"This *is* who I am." Theo's soft smile was radiant. "If I wanted to spend more time cavorting about in the sea, I would. But it's not harming me to stay a man. It only would hurt me if you had taken something that wasn't yours, or so I was always told. I'd grow melancholic and ill..." He cleared his throat. "Well, we saw a little glimpse of that when David pulled his little stunt. Didn't we?"

There had been evidence of the skin's absence, such as it was, in Theo's sluggishness and overall illness while the skin was hidden.

Still hesitant, Tom said, "You're certain?"

"Yes. Your concern does you credit, but I'm happy like this. Happier still to live here by the water."

Tom continued to gaze at him for some sign of concealed distress, knowing Theo was abominably clever at holding back what he wished to keep to himself. Theo murmured, "I'm happy with *you*. And with those we have gathered around us. I have no wish to spend my days as a seal."

"Wise," said a voice that was all rusty door hinges and dry autumn leaves. "Seals always seem fat and bored. Not that either is a bad state. But not much happens to them."

"Benson," said Theo, nodding a little in the direction past Tom's head.

Tom turned in his seat as Benson sailed to the bar, walked right behind it, and took his morning measure of gin. It was only moderately smaller than a full teacup's worth of liquid. "Utter cheek."

"Is Paul about?" Theo asked.

"Oh, he's about. I've just spoken to him. Now he's abed."

Fearing the worst, Tom said, "Is he in the same way as David was, or can we expect him to reappear today?" Knowing he hadn't imagined Alastair's way of speaking upon Paul's tongue, he expected his uncle was rather unwell.

After a long drink that set Tom to wincing, Benson said, "He'll be down by noon, I expect." He sat near the bar, about five or six feet from them.

"But when David—"

"David letting Alastair in was like tossing a log onto the fire." Tom wanted to clarify who was the fire and who was the log, but Benson was waving his arthritic free hand and still speaking. "He's got a flair for necromancy, hasn't he? The energies are similar between us—him—and the dead. The boundaries are permeable. Alastair could take more from David than David realized he was giving."

Narrowing his eyes, Tom said, "Benson, is it possible that you might have experience with that?"

But he was deft as a cat walking exactly where it shouldn't. It was, Tom felt, as good as a yes. "Paul seemed energized. He just hadn't slept all night because he was too busy talking to his, well, husband."

A thump sounded on the top of the bar, hollow

and loud, although no one else occupied the taproom. Theo raised his eyebrows and met Tom's eyes.

Benson just sighed. "Who, I've gathered, will be remaining with us for the foreseeable."

"The foreseeable?" Theo enquired.

"Mr. Gow and Mr. Apollyon reached another accord, apparently."

Running his fingers through his own hair as he watched Benson finish an amount of gin most sensible people only drank in the evening, and slowly at that, Tom said, "What kind of accord?"

Scoffing and scuffling, Benson grumbled, "It's very romantic."

"They always were," said Tom leniently. "What did they agree?"

"I'm sure Paul only told me because I might be subjected to his noise, seeing as I live here and all. Alastair'll come to him every night, if he wishes—" Benson made rather a show of glancing at the bar, near where they'd heard the thump. "And when Paul expires, which I doubt *I'll* be around for, Alastair will accompany him."

The meaning of it melted over Tom, sweet and slow. He started to grin as he felt its effect. "But you said... last night. You said he shouldn't keep Alastair here."

"Sometimes," said Benson, looking at neither of them, "I can be wrong."

"I don't know if you're wrong," said Theo, "if Paul isn't keeping Alastair here so much as the latter is simply *choosing* to be present."

Another thud came from the bar. It was, Tom imagined, an affirmative. "I reckon I can live with two uncles for a while," he said.

When they told David, David would probably cry

a little. He'd hide it, or try to, but he would be just as impacted. Lennie would be no less pleased.

"Isn't that something?" Theo marveled, his voice low.

Tom could think of nothing more fitting for the man who'd once lived in his own pub like a specter himself. What was more, he wanted happier years for all of them under this roof. In this moment, those years felt deliciously inevitable.

❧

THE WEEKEND after he'd taken a ghost to kill Ralph, David was drawn back to the pub where, really, the notion had all started. He didn't consider the lure mystical or magical; he merely missed his friends. *My family.* He also knew Theo and Tom would be itching to know what had transpired. Likewise, he wished to know if Alastair was still there or if Paul had somehow given him up at last. The prior felt more probable.

Between his need for physical rest and the little appointments that had surfaced because he'd been rather negligent of late, it had taken a few days to find the time to see everyone. When he walked into The Shuck again, it was with great relief and fondness. Cromer was bustling with energy, as it did during this season. Everyone seemed to be flinging themselves in all directions with good cheer, nattering about the pier, the almost-good weather, or food. Inside The Shuck, things were calm and quieter.

It didn't take long for Benson to say hello, though, as he materialized into view from the kitchen's direction.

"Have you ever considered you might only want to maintain one house?" Benson's question was affectionate, not dry or leading, and he even smiled at David, exposing his missing teeth.

"It's become a chief consideration, yes." David straightened his hat, something between a trilby and a boater that was perfect for summer. Consolidating and moving house had, as well as shifting some funds from the family business to this establishment. He might, however, have to force Paul to accept the latter. Lennie was advising him to wait until Tom had inherited.

"Things feel better with you here," Benson said, and it was as close to embracing David he would ever get. Before David could ask, he added. "He's upstairs, if you want to talk to him."

"Which him?" David would have spoken to anybody.

"Alastair."

"Where is Paul, then?" They were all but conjoined, really, even before Paul had offered himself up for possession.

"Down here, somewhere. Last I saw, the cellar."

"You seem far more relaxed about this haunting than you have been."

"I've decided," said Benson, drawing himself up so that he stood straight and speaking in a voice that brooked little argument or questioning, "this one is all right. One for the books, maybe, but nobody will suffer."

With a smile, for David agreed, he let Benson overtake him to a nook near the stairs and settle himself in an ugly leather armchair.

When David reached the landlord's flat, he knocked in a cursory fashion, too indoctrinated into the rules of politeness to halt them for someone who was dead.

"Come in," said Alastair. "I don't know why you're knocking, for one thing, since it's your flat."

Grinning, David opened the door and said, "It isn't, and I won't be rude just because you're a ghost." More of Paul's letters were littered throughout the parlor; Alastair stood with his hands on his hips amidst the paper-strewn furniture. "Getting in some good reading, I see."

"Paul is doing a stock take and that always takes ages, so I figured it wouldn't matter if things stayed messy up here. Anyway, he left 'em out for me. I can't move shit on my own." David noticed a couple of sheets that didn't bear Paul's hand. Glancing at one, he saw the sender had signed as Muriel. Alastair followed his gaze and smiled. "She's how *we* started. She and Abigail. I'm very glad she kept writing us after it was all over."

Eager, for he hadn't come upstairs to talk about something particular, David sat carefully on the few inches of sofa that weren't occupied by papers. He said, "Please do elaborate."

For the next fifteen minutes, David heard about Muriel, her lover Abigail, and exactly why Alastair had needed to hide in the cellar. He'd been delivering letters between the women, who were planning to run away, and was seen in Muriel's bedroom by Muriel's father, Sykes.

Sykes essentially chased Alastair to The Shuck, but couldn't catch him before Paul stepped in and furnished aid.

Enchanted, David asked when it seemed Alastair had reached a natural point of pause, "So they really did make it?"

"Hm?"

"They stayed together against... quite a few odds."

Alastair's happiness was tangible, and almost radiant rather than dreamy. "Oh yes," he said. "They settled in Edinburgh, actually, and when Paul finally wrote that her father was dead, Muriel said she preferred Scotland anyway and may as well stay. They're still there, I imagine, because not everyone has the misfortune of dying so young as me."

Marveling, gazing a little blankly at a small bouquet of flowers in a squat, carnelian hued vase, David said, "That's wonderful." He looked at Alastair. "Not your death, obviously, but their... marriage."

"I loved the idea," said Alastair, nodding. "It was what made me decide to ferry their letters in the first place. I'm a fucking romantic; I couldn't help it."

David sighed, more contentedly than anything. "Speaking of that..."

If Alastair was radiant a moment ago, he was presently incandescent. "I'm staying."

Given his joy, the meaning seemed plain enough to David. "You're a well enough behaved ghost, so I should think there will be no complaints."

"And whenever he leaves, I'll leave."

As a boy, this type of story would have caused David to dissolve into rapturous tears, ones he would have hidden from everybody so that he would not need to explain them. As he was, now, it filled him with serene delight. He did not know what to say, at first, such was the impact of even peaceful happiness. "I... in truth? I couldn't imagine a better idea for you two."

"Well," said Alastair, running a hand through his wild, long hair, "I'm glad you like it, because I should be thanking you."

The idea felt foreign, but David endeavored to become better at accepting thanks and owning his hand in others' joy. He thought it would be better to get used to it, rather than contribute to any chaos or destruction.

But because he could not find the right words, as ever, he merely blushed and tried to smile.

EPILOGUE
DECEMBER, 1930

"If there is anywhere on earth a lover of God who is always kept safe, I know nothing of it, for it was not shown to me. But this was shown: that in falling and rising again we are always kept in that same precious love." —Mother Julian of Norwich

Cromer

He supposed he could leave Cromer now. Whenever he gave the thought more than a moment's deliberation, he found a strange hesitancy dwelled in his heart. But today felt different for no reason at all, in the way an ordinary day deceptively could.

Time and politics had eroded Cromer's once notable reputation as a fashionable holiday destination, leaving it with a feeling that was rather stretched and lonely. Though it was certainly still a community, Theo had yet to see it return to its fin de siècle grandeur. He doubted it ever would, not after a war that had ripped through an entire generation and the later economic events that, likewise, impacted the world.

Although David still resided here, no one of his old set, if they were still in a condition to travel, bothered to visit as they once had. Its rhythms had changed, but when Theo stilled his mind and allowed his senses to reach deeper than he thought they could, he caught echoes of the life he'd once lived here.

He did not live in the cottage he still owned, choosing instead to let it to an unwed woman and her young son. He couldn't live there himself, for the echoes resonated most even when he did not try to hear them. Tom, always Tom, teasing him and uplifting him and making his hair stand on end. It was no ghost, not like Alastair had been, no shade lingering on this side of life because his lover needed it.

For that, Theo was grateful, as Tom deserved whatever restful thing came next. His life had been one of perpetual motion, so when he passed silently, early compared to many men, and without struggle—in bed like one of his uncles had—Theo could not have wished for a more peaceful resolution. Still, it had not been so peaceful for *him*.

Shortly after Tom died, he had to take up residence in The Shuck, where reminders of the past were rife but did not assault him like a cold wind bearing flecks of ice. He supposed they had more to do with Paul, or Paul and Alastair, who had—as Alastair intended—departed for their next life together. Or even Benson and Mrs. Lloyd.

All had left ink stains upon his heart. Their stains, however, were easier to confront than Tom's absence. Since David and Lennie were both cheerfully within this mortal coil, their presence went a long way toward easing Theo's spirit. Yet they could not assuage him entirely, and part of him felt lost. He believed it was a part that Tom had taken with him; he hadn't needed to give over his skin to Tom at all. The effect was the same.

Because Lennie and David were so much better at taking care of The Shuck than him, he gladly allowed them to do so. While he remained owner after the passing of the last two Apollyons, he did not behave as such, beyond tending to the relevant legalities and administrative tasks. David was technically landlord, having diverted money from his family's cloth business to this one well before Tom's death. It was just as well he did, for diversifying had only been in his best interests.

Theo's hand tightened around the slim sheaf of papers and they crinkled just slightly. If he was going to disappear, as his kind was liable to do, David would need these documents.

In his other hand, he held his skin less tightly.

Gazing out the little window at his view of the rain-drenched promenade, Theo decided today was to be his last one as a man. Readying himself to go downstairs, he barely glanced at his own reflection in the mirror. Tom would have chuckled at the preponderance of gray hair threaded in Theo's dark tresses, a thing that had only started to happen within the last couple of years and accelerated after he died.

Delayed aging was a dubious gift of Theo's preternatural state, not that he particularly wanted it. His years' collective weight was beginning to strain him, though. Even if nobody—even a seer, unless they saw something incredibly specific—could know exactly when they'd expire, he suspected he was nearing the end of his rather long life. There was a slow, weighted sensation to everything now.

Even going down flights of these familiar and slightly uneven stairs was, at his age, an exercise in caution. He found David at the foot of them, putting away a ledger behind the old desk they still used as a reception area. He muttered to himself about something Theo could not catch.

Smiling, Theo cleared his throat and David turned around, quizzical expression making him look for all the world like the same pretty, rather staid man Theo had loved at the start.

His clothes were different, not nearly as intricate as anything they'd all favored at the start of this century, yet he still preferred his jumpers in the same jewel tones as he had his suits. There were more wrinkles about his angular face and blue eyes. But age had refined him rather than worn him down, much like Lennie had softened his edges and built him up.

The quizzical air soon gave way to something more troubled, as though David could divine what was on Theo's mind. Maybe he could, although the talent had never been one of his own when it came to anybody living. He glanced at the skin in Theo's hand. Lennie, perhaps, could come closer to actually reading Theo's thoughts, but they were nowhere to be seen. Mornings were not their favorite time to be functional.

Maybe that was just as well. Theo did not like goodbyes. He might be tempted to linger here if he had to furnish them, which would probably only lead to someone he loved finding him dead in his rooms within the best scenario. There'd been enough of that in this pub.

Whether it was right or not, he preferred his way of leaving. He held out the array of papers. "Here, old chap."

"What're these?"

Softly, Theo said, looking into his eyes, "You know

what they are. I can't just disappear without leaving them, or you and Lennie would be faced with a rather complicated situation, wouldn't you?"

In reply to that, it seemed, David took them, the deed and various other legal papers, with a huff. "When aren't we?"

"Well, legally. The owner of your building just, what, melts away? The authorities might think you murdered me and *then* where would you be? This way, you can file everything seamlessly. I've transferred ownership to you already; it's all signed and ready. There's also the cottage, too. You own it, as well."

He thought of Miss Fraser and her child, a bright little lad called Michael. He wouldn't want anyone to cast them out, and David would never.

David's mouth quirked into half a smile with apparent reluctance. "Where will you go?"

"To the water."

"And then?"

"I don't know." It was the truth. He didn't know at all, and having not changed for years, he half-wondered if the effort might stretch him too thin. But he felt the risk was acceptable.

"I'll miss you."

Theo took his free hand and held it. "I know." He thought of what David had to anchor him and tried to explain his own underlying rationale. "But you'll still have a tether here." It had been a year since Tom had left, yet one felt like thirty.

Lennie and David were family; he loved them dearly and no less than Tom. Nonetheless, they couldn't be expected to make up for such stark collective absences. Theo was older, and so his own losses had amounted to such a point that, combined with the mounting effects of age itself, he was simply exhausted.

Giving him a nod and an astute look, David said, "You don't need to explain it to me. Just know, we love you. I love you. Always did, even if I botched it."

"You didn't entirely." If he had, he'd more than made up for it.

"*If* you come back, you always have a place here."

That meant more to Theo than other promises ever could.

He smiled, thinking of the occasions when he'd joined Lennie or David, or Lennie and David, in bed. Tom had been slightly less inclined to participate and didn't always, although he did always enjoy watching and offering delicious commentary. Their respective pairs remained within this arrangement, which they'd all agreed upon without any ill feelings. David lived with Lennie; Theo with Tom.

Once, in confidence while serving him a dram in the taproom, Lennie told Theo they couldn't imagine everyone cohabitating—but that was Tom and David's fault. Theo had guffawed so loudly, David glanced up from his seat and asked what was so funny.

The unashamed expressions of affection were warm, and beneficial to their understandings of each other. They were love incarnate, and communicative besides. So Theo did not need to say he felt a return was unlikely, or that he almost felt as though, instead of becoming a seal, he might well dissolve into foam.

David couldn't be expected to bear those things. Judging by his expression, Theo suspected he was already thinking them. Or something similarly grim and poetic.

Casting a careful eye to the foyer—not that it was a proper foyer or ever had been one—and knowing it was empty of anybody who might take offense, Theo kissed him on the lips. "Thank you."

After a small smile and gentle return of the kiss, David murmured, "Of course."

Then Theo left him, knowing David would go to a window and watch Theo walk away into the rain.

It was a cold day, but that mattered little. Once he was a seal or sea foam, if that was what fate decided to do with him, he would not feel it so keenly. The beach was devoid of people, loud with the slap of water upon water, and painted in shades of umber and iron.

Carefully he made his way to the edge of the tide, further out than most people would dare go. He waited for a wave to inundate him to the waist, then the chest. By the third that crashed around him, he was submerged. He didn't change, yet.

Theo let go, felt his feet lose contact with the sand as water buoyed him up and filled his nostrils. The sound was muted here, even though the rush of water was strong to his senses. He did what Tom could not—or what he would not allow Tom to do—all those years prior, and slipped into the sea, more serene than Tom had ever been.

It might have been the cold or the stormy conditions playing tricks on his perception, or perhaps he was as exhausted as he suspected. He would have sworn Tom lingered just out of reach, arms outstretched as though to meet him.

The man had given the skin back. Repeatedly, and without ulterior motive. But he still kept the selkie.

ALSO BY CAMILLE DUPLESSIS

Threads of Wyrd

The Kraken and The Canary

Like Silk Breathing

The Only Story

Unfair Winds

ABOUT THE AUTHOR

Camille is a thalassophile who sadly spent too long residing in Chicago, where there's just a very large lake and no sea. An enquiring and possibly over-educated mind, she's been described as "the politest contrarian." Though everyone believes she's tall, she's not. Likewise, she doesn't dress in all-black.